WICKED ATTRACTION

Novels by Marie Rochelle
Published by Phaze Books

Alpha Male Incorporated: Under Your Protection
Alpha Male Incorporated: Access Granted
A Taste of Love: Richard
Closer to You: Lee
My Deepest Love: Zack
More Than Friends: Brad
Caught
Caught 2: Ajana's Return
Desire
All the Fixin'
Crossing the Railroad
A Rancher's Promise
The Men of CCD: Slow Seduction
The Men of CCD: Loving True
The Men of CCD: Help Wanted
Lucky Charms
Hunks: Too Hot to Touch
Hunks: Opposite Attraction
Hunks: Pulled Over
Me & Mrs. Jones
Taken by Storm
Tempting Turner
Roped Into You
So Much Better
Bikers & Bars: Dante's Way
Sinful
Tough to Love
Unexpected Lover
After Hours
Wicked Attraction

WICKED ATTRACTION

MARIE ROCHELLE

East Baton Rouge Parish Library
Baton Rouge, Louisiana

Wicked Attraction Copyright © 2014 by Marie Rochelle
ALL RIGHTS RESERVED.

Edited by Kathryn Lively
Cover Art © 2014 by Fiona Jayde

First Mundania Edition February 2014
Trade Paperback ISBN: 978-1-60659-752-1
eBook ISBN: 978-1-60659-693-7

Published by Phaze Books
An imprint of Celeritas Unlimited LLC
6457 Glenway Ave., #109
Cincinnati, OH 45211

All rights reserved under the International and Pan-American Copyright Conventions. No part of this book may be reproduced or transmitted in any form or by any means, electronic or mechanical including photocopying, recording, or by any information storage and retrieval system, without permission in writing from the publisher, Celeritas Unlimited LLC, 6457 Glenway Avenue, #109, Cincinnati, Ohio 45211, books@mundania.com.

This book is a work of fiction. Names, characters, places and incidents are either the product of the author's imagination or are used fictitiously, and any resemblance to any actual persons, living or dead, events, or locales is entirely coincidental. The publisher does not have any control over and does not assume any responsibility for author or third-party websites or their content.

Legal File Usage—Your eBook Rights
Payment of the download fee for the ebook edition of this book grants the purchaser the right to download and read this file on any devices the purchaser owns, and to maintain private backup copies of the file for the purchaser's personal use only. It is a violation of copyright law for the purchaser to share or redistribute the ebook edition of this book to anyone who has not purchased the eBook.

The unauthorized reproduction or distribution of this or any copyrighted work is illegal. Authors are paid on a per-purchase basis. Any use of this file beyond the rights stated above constitutes theft of the author's earnings. File sharing is an international crime, prosecuted by the United States Department of Justice Division of Cyber Crimes, in partnership with Interpol. Criminal copyright infringement, including infringement without monetary gain, is punishable by seizure of computers, up to five years in federal prison and a fine of $250,000 per reported instance. Please purchase only authorized electronic or print editions and do not participate in or encourage the electronic piracy of copyrighted material. Your support of the author's rights and livelihood is appreciated.

Production by Celeritas Unlimited LLC
Printed in the United States of America
10 9 8 7 6 5 4 3 2 1

Dedication:

*Believe everyday
is the best day
of the year.*

Chapter One

Jaleena Falcon drove down the street, trying to fight off the bitter disappointment after leaving the flea market empty handed. It had been over three weeks since she found anything worthwhile at any of her favorite hot spots. She had woken up early and drove two hours for absolutely *nothing*.

She had to find some good pieces for her store, but it wasn't happening for her. Her latest hunt turned up zilch, and she was running out of ideas. She couldn't afford to make another trip back home without something in the back of her truck. She couldn't describe the pleasure she got from purchasing dusty and outdated pieces of furniture no one else wanted or took a second look at, then turning them into treasures to sell at her business.

Turning the corner, Jaleena was headed towards her store when a beautiful item that had been tossed on the side of the road captured her attention. *This must be my lucky day.* She must have done something right this morning, because she couldn't believe what she saw.

Sure, she was good at finding things at the flea market,

but nothing ever appeared out of nowhere for her. Jaleena truly believed her days of finding good deals were over after her horrible morning. She had given up all hope for discovering a diamond in the rough. Still, it seemed like someone loved her more than she first thought, since things were improving for her. She couldn't be more excited if there was a pile of money lying in the middle of the empty highway.

Not twenty feet in front of her was a gorgeous black loveseat, or divan as more fashion forward people might call it, with a note taped to it with the word *Free*. In the past, Jaleena had been fortunate enough to find abandoned pieces, but *never* anything that looked this brand new. It looked like it came from a showroom of any major furniture store in town.

Driving past the divan, she parked her truck and rushed over to the item of her dreams. She crossed her fingers that there weren't any surprises waiting for her that she couldn't see from a distance. If the first glance turned out the way she hoped and prayed, Jaleena found the last piece for her grand opening tomorrow.

Bending down, she felt her skinny jeans stretch across her ass and, in the back of her mind, she could hear her mother saying *Jaleena, girl, you know better than to wear pants that tight. You don't need to advertise everything that you have.* She quickly shoved the memory of her amazing mother away. She didn't want to start crying, not when she had so much work to do.

Reaching out, she ran her hands over the material, checking it for any signs of damage, but she didn't see a thing wrong with it. She was astonished someone would just toss away expensive furniture for no apparent reason.

What was that old saying? *Someone else's junk is another*

person's treasure.

Hell, she had found a gem in this and she wasn't about to leave it here for another person to take. This would bring in an excellent price at her business, *Talk of the Town.*

Dashing back to her truck, Jaleena backed it up until the lift she had installed on it was in front of the divan. It was like a tow truck, but only for furniture and other pieces she couldn't move on her own or without some extra help. Operating the controls on the console inside her vehicle, she moved it and placed it in the back without any problems.

Jaleena glanced in the rearview mirror and made sure there weren't any cars coming before pulling off the side of the road and back into the street. As she drove towards her store, she couldn't help but remember the main reason she started *Talk of the Town* in the first place—her wonderful mother.

Her dreams of owning something that she could call her own came to her when she was a little girl. Every Saturday morning her mother would wake up early for their weekly visits to rummage sales. Going out and doing that with her parent was, without a doubt, the favorite part of her weekend. It seemed like the week couldn't go by fast enough for her back then.

Yet, like clockwork at seven o'clock on Saturday morning, her mother would holler upstairs at her. "Jaleena, you better be up and dressed if you want to go with me. You know that I will leave without you." She actually knew that her mama would wait for her, but she liked giving Jaleena that little threat to get her moving a little faster, and it worked every single time.

What her mother didn't realize was she was already dressed and about to race down the stairs. She loved riding her pink Huffy bicycle with the white basket tied on the handlebars, and it would be outside waiting for her.

Laughing to herself, Jaleena ran her fingers through her hair and recalled how she loved learning the ropes of being a good second-hand shopper. Back then, she studied very closely how her mama would check each and every item quite well to make sure of its condition.

The best rummage sales were the ones where they found plenty of things at good to great prices. If the seller didn't like to bargain with her mama, then she would just leave the item there and walk away. Most of the time people wanted the sale, so they went down to the price her mama offered them.

Jaleena also learned something else as a child. She watched the ladies wearing huge diamond rings on their fingers. She saw how they picked items that looked inexpensive and one day she overheard a few of them talking to each other. God, she learned so much about her future job by going to those amazing rummage sales with her mother.

"Mama, I miss you so much," Jaleena sighed as she continued thinking about her past. "I wish that you were still here with me. We could be working side by side."

She had been best friends with her mother and it had devastated her beyond belief when she passed away. In spite of that, she *knew* her loving mother was smiling down from Heaven, because her baby girl made her business dreams finally come true at the age of twenty-eight.

I swear that I'm going to continue to make you proud of me, Jaleena told herself. *Talk of the Town* was as much her inspiration as well as her mother's, and she wasn't about to let it fail for the either of them.

CHAPTER TWO

Across town, Ridge Taylor slipped hurriedly into his pants and was looking for a shirt inside his closet when a pair of hands wrapped around his waist and ran up and down his bare chest. He didn't even have to guess who it was...it was *her*!

Why did he keep falling back into her games? It was time...beyond time for him to move on from her clinging ways, but she didn't seem to know how to let him go.

"Caitlin, do you still have a key to my house? I thought I had taken it back from you last week. You can't just walk into my home anytime you feel like it. How many times have I told you to knock and wait for me to answer?"

"Baby, I did knock on the front door twice, but you must have been in the shower and didn't hear me," she whined, playing with the button on his jeans. "I missed you. Haven't you missed me, too? I only came by to see if you wanted to have dinner with me tonight."

Grabbing a shirt out of the closet, Ridge brushed Caitlin's unwanted touch off his body and stepped away from her. He had dated Caitlin Alexander on and off for a few months, but he never wished to commit to her. They both only wanted to have some fun, and it always stayed like that for him.

Yet, she couldn't seem to understand that.

Sure, the sex had been great at first, but now he was looking for something more…with substance. All Caitlin wanted him to do was stay in her bedroom twenty-four hours, seven days a week. He wasn't the type of man to be kept by any woman, especially a wealthy one.

He had a job, and he loved working at his family business as a plumber. Still, Caitlin acted like she never believed the words coming out of his mouth, and he was tired of repeating himself to her. It was like she was difficult on purpose.

He should have listened to Billy when he had the chance a few months back, and now he was caught up in a situation he couldn't get out of. His grandfather warned him once about getting involved with an older woman, because Caitlin might become possessive of him and the time they spent together, but he ignored the advice.

Back then he didn't think their nine-year age difference would matter that much. It wasn't like she was old enough to be his mother or anything. He was thirty-four and Caitlin was only forty-five. He made the awful mistake of thinking they had gone into this relationship with their eyes wide open, but now he saw how wrong he was.

Caitlin didn't want to leave him alone. She wanted to be in his life *forever* and wasn't about to let him leave her for any reason. He was running out of ways to tell her in a nice way that they weren't a couple anymore.

Why can't she move on and find someone to hover over besides me?

Honestly, in his opinion, she could have any man she set her sights on, yet it seemed like she was hooked only on him. It wasn't like Caitlin wasn't a stunning woman with her flame red hair, dark green eyes, and tall, athletic runner's body. He had mentioned to her a couple of times that she couldn't get any skinnier, but his comments went in one ear and right out of the other, so he just stopped saying it. Caitlin insisted the thinner she was the prettier she looked to everyone else. She got off on people envying the way she looked. It made her feel so superior to them.

"Hey, there's no need to get dressed now since I'm here." She snatched the shirt out of his hands and tossed it on the bed. Then she eased around the front of him and stared up into his eyes. "Why don't I show you how happy I am to see you? I promise I can make you feel good."

She reached for his zipper and started pulling it down. "Baby, I missed you so much. I'm so glad that I caught you at home." Caitlin tried kissing him on the mouth, but he quickly turned his head so it landed on his cheek instead.

He didn't want to hurt her feelings by being mean or rude, but he truly wasn't interested in a sexual relationship with her anymore. He liked his women into him, yet Caitlin had gone overboard with her constant affections. It almost came across now as neediness on her part. Hell, it was borderline obsession and he couldn't let it go any further. "Caitlin, haven't I told you time and time again it's over between us? You can't keep doing this." Placing his hands on her shoulders, Ridge gently moved Caitlin away from him. He quickly zipped his pants, grabbed his shirt off the bed, and put it on.

"I'm hungry and was about to grab something to eat. Do you want to come with me? I think we really need to talk about us again," he asked. "I haven't gotten through to you the last three times we spoke about this."

It was now or never. Ridge had to get Caitlin to understand that they weren't exclusive anymore. She could go her way and he could go his. They both needed to find someone new. Sadly, a part of him thought they could at least be friends, but he saw now that wasn't even a possibility.

He was trying his best to make the split between them a painless experience so they could both walk away without having any bad feelings for each other.

Yet, she made it very hard for him to like the sight of her. She was always there in his face, bothering him when he wasn't interested in seeing her, or hearing her ask him for sex.

Caitlin glared at him like he was insane. "Fine, I'll go to lunch with you because I've missed you. I do not believe you when you tell me that things are over. God, I mean, we are so good together. Do you see how we turn heads every time I take you to an event? All of my girlfriends are jealous that I have someone as gorgeous as you on my arm. Why would I ever let you go?"

Ridge decided not to get into an argument about this inside his house. A place full of people would be better to finally make Caitlin understand that he meant business about them being over. Grabbing Caitlin's hand, he led her from his bedroom. "Come on, I'll take you to that Chinese restaurant you love so much."

∽·∾

"Whew!" Jaleena sighed as she made it into the coolness of her shop and out of the blazing hot sun. She never thought that she would to make it back here in time.

Sometimes it seemed like the drive from her flea market trips back to *Talk of the Town* took longer and longer each time she went.

"Trent? Trent...where are you?"

She knew her brother was in here somewhere. *So, where in the hell is he?* She shouldn't have given him the spare key after all of the trouble he had been involved in, but he was her family. She was holding out hope that this might be the time he would change his ways. Since their mother was gone, all they had was each other. She hoped Trent wasn't abusing the little trust she still had for him by stealing anything from her.

It took a few minutes before her brother came from the back of her shop with food in his hand.

"Fuck, why are you constantly screaming my name? I'm not deaf. I can hear you just fine," her brother shouted, glaring at her. He took a huge bite of the sandwich in his hand.

"Trent, I don't have time for your attitude today," she snapped back. "I need you to help me with this new piece of furniture. I can't move it by myself into the store."

"*What?*" Trent uttered around a huge bite of sandwich in his mouth. "Why do I always have to help you? What kind of crap have you dragged here now? Why can't you buy it new and then resell it? You got half of our mama's money from her estate when she died. You don't have to put used junk in here. I thought you would be smarter than to invest in this shit hole of a place."

The nerve of him! How dare her lazy ass brother think he could talk to her like this!

Jaleena was so tired of Trent and his nasty attitude towards her. He was clearly jealous because she had done something with her life.

"Shut up, Trent. Why is it my fault that you didn't know to use the money Mama left us? It isn't my fault you wasted your half on anything and everything. I bought this little shop because it was my dream. Why didn't you make a better investment with your half?"

"There you go with that blame shit," Trent shouted at her. "You were always Mama's favorite anyway, because of those yard sales. You always went with her, but I never got invited along. You were constantly getting special treatment and I was abandoned."

Jaleena couldn't believe Trent tried to pull this shit with her. He knew the reason their mother stopped taking him. "The couple of times she did, you stole things. Stealing at a garage sale is ridiculous, and that's why Mama started leaving you at home. She shouldn't have had to worry about keeping an eye on you. It was wrong for you to even put her in that position in the first place."

"I wasn't really stealing," Trent complained, pointing a finger at her. "Hell, it was a yard sale. It wasn't like they were going to miss any of that crap. All of these second-hand goods remind me of the places that Mama used to take you. I thought the stuff you came back home with was worthless back then and it still is now."

That's it! She wasn't going to deal with her ungrateful brother anymore. She could find someone else to help her get the divan out of the back of the truck. Trent wouldn't do anything but complain the whole time, anyway.

"Get out! Get out now!" Jaleena screamed at her brother. "I only allowed you to come here after you got out of jail because of Mama. Honestly, I didn't want anything to do with you and all of your excuses."

"Stop acting so over-the-top," Trent sighed, rolling his

eyes. "Why don't you get your shit together and act your age?"

Anger swept through Jaleena's body at her brother's insults. Why in the hell was he telling her to get her shit together? Half the time he didn't have two pennies to rub together, and wasn't he the one who got sent away to prison instead of doing the smart thing and cutting a deal like his so-called friends had done? Better yet, not committing a crime in the first place?

"Trent, you need to watch what you say to me, because you know that eventually you'll be begging for my help like you always do. Next time, I might leave your ass out to dry."

Her brother moved closer in a menacing manner until his chest almost was touching hers. "You aren't strong enough to do that. You don't know how to say no to me. You're just like our mother. She always threatened to not get me out of trouble, but ended up doing it every time I came to her. You're cut from the same cloth, so learn to deal with it." Trent smirked at her before taking a huge bite out of his sandwich.

Jaleena felt her blood racing through her veins as Trent insulted the memory of their loving mother. She fought the urge to slap the taste out of his mouth. Taking a deep breath, she tried to calm herself down. She didn't want to end up getting arrested for kicking her brother's ungrateful ass.

"Did you even think about leaving me any food in the refrigerator for my upcoming opening?"

"I wasn't thinking about you when I was making this," Trent said, waving the food in her face.

"God, take that sandwich and get the hell out of my sight before I do something I might regret later. Oh, by the way, I hope you enjoy every damn bite because believe this:

it will be the last fucking thing you will get from me. Now, get out of my store."

Trent's gaze swung down to the sandwich in his hand before shooting a hateful look in her direction. "I don't know who the fuck you think you are, but you don't talk to me like that! Take this damn sandwich. I don't need it," he snapped, throwing the food at her.

Jaleena jumped back just before the food hit her in the chest. *Oh, no, he didn't just throw that food at me!*

She had this place all clean and her brother wasn't going to mess it up. "Stop acting like a bastard!" she yelled. "You better pick that sandwich up and toss it in the trash."

Her brother narrowed his hazel eyes at her as a dark look came over his face. "Fine, I'll clean it up, but you won't like how I get rid of it."

Reaching down, Trent snatched up the remains of the half-eaten sandwich, spun around on his heel, and rushed in the direction of the bathroom. Seconds later, she heard a loud splash and then her brother yelled out from the other room at her. "There, I got rid of it. Are you happy now?"

Jaleena stood in shock as she heard the toilet flush, and she raced into the bathroom. She got there just in time to see the thick sandwich trying to go down, but it kept floating around in the toilet and she knew it was clogged.

"Look at what you did!" she hollered, hitting her brother in the shoulder.

She grabbed the soggy remains of the sandwich out of the toilet and threw it at Trent. "I can't believe you just did this shit to me. Hand me that plunger. You better pray I will be able to fix this."

Trent wiped the food off his clothing. "If you weren't my baby sister, I would knock the living shit out of you, throwing food from the toilet on me. But, I know you would call the cops on me and have me tossed back into jail."

Shoving past her, Trent tossed her a dirty look. "I don't see a plunger. So, I guess you're out of luck, little sister," he snickered as he left her alone in the bathroom.

"I don't believe you." Jaleena went over to the other side of the toilet and searched for the plunger, but it was nowhere in sight. It had to be there. She just got a new one yesterday and placed it right here. Where did it go?

"Trent, I know you did something with that plunger. Why are you purposely trying to ruin the most important week of my life? Give me back the plunger and get out like I have been telling you." She followed her brother to the front of the store. "I'm not going to waste the rest of my day dealing with your behavior."

"I didn't touch that thing. What in the hell would I need with it? Maybe it's stuck in your ass and that's why you're such a bitch to me all of the time."

Jaleena wouldn't get into another argument with Trent. He constantly found ways to push her buttons. Since she knew he was lying to her and would keep lying, she had to find a plumber and see if he would be able to fix the toilet. She remembered cutting an ad out of the newspaper yesterday and placing it somewhere in her office.

Going around Trent, she made her way to her back office. Standing next to her desk, she stared at the pile of papers on it.

"I know I tossed that newspaper clipping here. I hope I can find it and they can help me. If I can't, tomorrow is going to be ruined for me." She moved papers around on the surface until she found it.

"Thank God," Jaleena sighed as she picked up the clipping and read it out loud:

Taylor's Plumbing
24-Hour Plumbing Service
We can fix any problem, big or small.
Excellent Rates

"I hope they are good as their ad," she mumbled to herself before grabbing the phone and dialing the phone number. It rang at least four times, and she was about to hang up when a male voice finally answered.

"Taylor's Plumbing. Billy speaking, how may I help you?" he asked in a professional manner.

Jaleena almost jumped for joy at getting a live voice and not an answering machine. "Yes, I'm calling about your ad. I'm having a serious problem with my toilet. Do you think you can come out and help me? I mean, it's really bad."

"What kind of problem, miss?" the man inquired.

"My brother flushed food down it, and now it's overflowing."

"Did you try using a plunger? Maybe that will get it out for you?" he suggested. "I want to get a feel for what you might have already done before I send a man out there."

"I don't have a plunger, so I'm in desperate need of help. Can you please send someone?" Jaleena knew she was practically begging for help and she didn't give a damn.

"I think I can get someone out there to see you, but I can't guarantee when they'll come. All of our plumbers are out on other jobs at the moment."

"Sir, I'm having an open house tomorrow for my new business. Please try to find someone. I really need this bathroom fixed and your ad does say you are open twenty-hours.

Can't you find anyone to come here and fix my problem now?" Jaleena glanced over her shoulder as Trent strolled into her office looking smug. She didn't have time to deal with his nonsense.

"Miss, calm down," the guy said softly, as though trying to soothe her nerves. "Yes, I can send someone over there today. Give me your address and I'll get him to you ASAP."

"My address is 521 Johnson Street. It's a small furniture store on the left hand side. It's called *Talk of the Town*."

"Okay, hang tight. I should have him there in an hour, maybe less. I know it's a Saturday afternoon, but someone will be there."

"Wonderful, I'll be here," Jaleena told the guy before she hung up.

"I can't believe you're throwing such a fit," Trent complained, glaring at her.

"Listen, you better hope this guy can fix my toilet or you're going to be in a lot of trouble with me," Jaleena threatened, her eyes narrowing at her brother.

Trent came across the room and got directly in her face. The cold look in his eyes sent a chill down her spine. "Jaleena, you're my sister, but I'm getting tired of your threats. You better stop it now or you won't like the outcome at all."

Jaleena swallowed hard, trying to think of a way to get Trent out of her shop, but nothing was coming to mind. She shouldn't be terrified of her brother, yet she was. The time he spent locked up had changed him, and it wasn't for the better.

Chapter Three

"You know that I loathe going to the movies, but you always take me to those things," Caitlin grumbled, staring at him across the table. They had to leave the movie early because of her complaining.

"Caitlin, you knew when you started dating me that I like to go to the movies in my free time. Why are you acting like this is a surprise all of a sudden?" Ridge asked, glancing at his watch and thinking of a way to get rid of her. "Besides, I told you I wanted to see that movie before our date, you were the one who invited yourself. Don't blame me for your not having a good time. It was your fault, not mine."

"Well, I didn't like it and I wanted to leave," she mumbled. "Why are you acting so mad at me?"

God, he really had to get rid of her before she gave him gray hair. "Didn't we leave early? That should make you feel good. Now, I have to go back later by myself to see how it ends."

"You do remember that I wanted you to be my date for the Mayor's Ball on New Year's Day," Caitlin continued like he hadn't even spoken a word. "I already have the perfect tuxedo picked out for you. You're going to love it. It will look amazing on your body."

Ridge could barely hold his temper in check as he glared across the table at Caitlin. "No, Caitlin. I have told you, stop trying to put me in situations with your friends. It's not me and I don't like being around them. Can't you comprehend that we aren't together anymore? What else can I do to make you realize that?"

"Well, Mayor Greenwell's money wasn't too horrific for you to take last week when you fixed his sink. So, what is the big deal about being my date for this party? Everyone knows that we're a couple," Caitlin said. "Why are you trying to deny what we feel for each other? I don't care about the age difference. You shouldn't feel embarrassed by it, either. The whole town thinks we are practically living together."

"I don't care what the whole town thinks. This is the last time we're going to be seen out together. We have both outgrown each other and it's about time you realize it. We need to go our separate ways." Ridge prayed that Caitlin finally dropped her fantasy about them being together forever because he didn't know if he could be any nicer to her.

Caitlin gave him a strange look, and he could tell from the expression on her face that she was about to say something. However, his cell phone started ringing and thankfully cut off whatever she was going to tell him. Ridge silently praised the person on the other end before he answered it.

"Ridge speaking," he said into the phone.

"Ridge, I hate to bother you. I know you were going to the movies," Billy said.

"Billy, what is it?" He hoped it was something that would take him away from Caitlin. The situation was getting out of hand so fast.

"We got a call at 521 Johnson Street. A woman called about a problem with her toilet. Do you think you can go and take a look at it? I would go myself, but there's nobody here to answer the phones."

Ridge looked at Caitlin and saw the determined look in her eyes. She wasn't about to give him a break about the mayor's party. He had to get out of here before he said something he wouldn't be able to take back. One thing he couldn't stand was a *needy* woman—when it came to that "one" word, she was at the top of the list.

"That's not a problem. I'll leave right now. I have all the equipment I need in the truck. Thanks for the phone call, Billy." Disconnecting, Ridge shoved the phone into his back jeans pocket. Caitlin was going to be pissed at him.

"That was Billy on the phone. There's a plumbing problem I need to take care of. I need to leave." Ridge stood, hoping to make a fast exit without Caitlin giving him any problems.

"Okay. I hope you can get it fixed, but don't forget to give me a call later." She looked at him like she really wanted to argue with him.

"Sure," Ridge responded, and then rushed out of the building. He wasn't about to call her about anything ever again.

Chapter Four

Jaleena was fed up with Trent thinking he could treat her horribly because he was the oldest. He might not think she had a backbone, but she did and would fight back if he pushed her far enough with his nasty ass attitude. She didn't know why he was still here. He wasn't helping her at all. The only thing he knew how to do well was make her life more difficult.

"Trent, I think you should leave. You've done more than enough destruction for one day. Honestly, I'm not sure if I even want to see your face again in my store."

Her mother raised her to love her brother, but this was the final straw. Trent wasn't going to ruin her dreams because he'd made bad decisions that affected him for the worse. She wouldn't allow his poison to spill over into her life.

Trent yanked her roughly by her upper arm and jerked her against his body. "I'm so fucking tired of you acting like you are so much better than me! You aren't the precious little princess Mama made you think you are. You're just like anyone else."

"Stop it, Trent! Let go of my arm." Jaleena tried wrestling her arm away, but her brother wouldn't let go.

"No!"

"What in the hell is wrong with you today? I know you can get in these moods, but today is the worst. Don't you know that you may have ruined my grand opening tomorrow?" She tried not to flinch as her brother's fingers dug into her arm.

"I need some money," Trent said.

She should have known that he would be asking her for money. Trent wouldn't know the meaning of an honest day of work if his life depended on it. Her initial fears were correct—he was probably looking for money in the store and intended to steal it. She couldn't trust him, no matter how much she wanted to get him another chance. Her brother might be family, but he wasn't going to change.

"Money...why do you need that?" she questioned.

"I need a thousand dollars. Give it to me and I'll leave you alone."

"A thousand dollars?" Jaleena gasped, stunned by the amount. "Have you lost your mind? You were given seven thousand dollars from Mama's estate. What did you do with all of that? Did you waste it on drugs or cheap women?"

Anger flashed in Trent's light brown eyes. He actually looked like he was about to strike her until he got himself under control. "I made some bad investments. That's all. Now be a good little sister and give me the money. I just need a thousand dollars. Damn it! I know you have it. You never spend anything. I'm really surprised you spent any money at all on this dump."

Jaleena quickly swallowed her nasty retort as it worked its way up her throat. She didn't need to piss off her brother any more than he already was. Trent had a bad temper—however, he wasn't going to bully her into giving him that money, either. He made his bed and now he would to have to lie in it.

"No, I'm not giving you any money," she said, trying to twist away from him again. "Get your hands off me and leave me the hell alone."

⁂

Ridge knew that the two people engaged in a heated discussion didn't sense him standing there watching them. He couldn't believe how the guy manhandled the woman. He wasn't going to let him keep doing this to her. The guy had to be at least six feet, three inches compared to the woman's smaller height.

"Did you not hear what the lady said?" Ridge demanded, coming further into the office. He moved his work bag off his shoulder as he tried to keep his cool.

Their heads spun around in his direction at the sound of his voice. He felt like he had gotten punched in the stomach when his eyes connected with the woman's. Her eyes were such a dark brown that they almost looked black. Long, spiral curls brushed her milk chocolate shoulders. She looked at him and then back at the guy with the death grip on her arm.

For some reason he felt an undeniable rage and wanted to kill that guy for putting his hands on her like that. She was trying to pretend that she wasn't in pain, but he could see the discomfort shining in her beautiful eyes.

"Who in the hell do you think you are, telling me what to do?" the guy snarled at him.

"I'm the plumber. I got a call about something being

lodged inside of the toilet. I called out a few times when I came in. But, I doubt either one of you could hear me above the screaming," Ridge replied, still glaring at the guy.

"Do you mind letting me go now? I think you've gotten your point across," the female said, staring at him then back up at the guy with the death grip of her arm.

"You can't tell me what to do. Who in the fuck do you think you are?"

Ridge tried to keep calm, but the guy was starting to piss him off. "I think you're hurting her. Don't you see the pain in her eyes?"

He couldn't tear his gaze away from the woman's striking face. Of course, he had noticed black women before and always found them very attractive, but the woman in front of him was truly breathtaking.

The guy eyed him like he was sizing him up. "Did she tell you she was in pain?"

"Trent, please let go of my arm." The softness in the woman's voice made Ridge's gut clench. It was like music to his ears.

"Jaleena, are you going to give me the money or not?" Trent asked, releasing her arm.

"There's some money under the counter out front. It's in a metal box. That's all the money I have, and after you take it I want you out of here. I mean it, don't step a foot in my place again."

Ridge watched how Jaleena rubbed the upper part of her arm and he suppressed the urge to hit Trent in his face. They were almost the same height, but he definitely had a muscle advantage on the younger man. He didn't know Jaleena, but the desire to protect her was strong, and he would act on it if the guy touched her again.

"I'll take that, but I know it isn't going to be enough." Trent brushed past Jaleena and tossed him a threatening look before storming out of the office.

A second or two later the slam of the front door echoed through the building. Ridge was pleased Trent was finally gone, or else something would have happened because of the way he treated Jaleena.

"Sorry you had to see that," Jaleena apologized. "I'm glad you came in, because my brother might have never left." She tried to give him a small smile to ease the tension in the room, but it didn't work.

The guy who was about to beat up Jaleena was her own brother? What in the world was wrong with him? Weren't siblings supposed to protect and not harm each other?

"Does he always treat you like that?" He didn't want to be nosy, but Ridge couldn't tolerate any man who abused a woman. Jaleena might not have had a chance against her brother if he hadn't come in here.

"Trent hasn't had the best of luck and he feels like the world owes him."

"Isn't that going to make life even harder on him?" he questioned. "I mean, there are a lot of people in this world. I'm sure some of them are going to tell him 'no' more than once."

Jaleena's eyes sparkled as though she found his comment funny. "I think I'm going to like you a lot, Mister....?"

Stepping forward, Ridge extended his hand. "Ridge Taylor," he said. "It's very nice to meet you."

"Jaleena Falcon. It's very nice to meet you, too," Jaleena said, shaking his hand and letting it go sooner than he wanted. He loved how soft her skin was. "I hope that you can fix the problem with my toilet. I can't believe he did this to me out of spite. Trent knows how much tomorrow means to me."

"I haven't met a problem toilet that I couldn't fix." Ridge grinned, not knowing what it was doing to the woman in front of him.

⁂

Jaleena tried her best not to notice how sexy, tall, and handsome Ridge was. The gray sleeveless shirt he wore stretched across his chest, displaying his toned, tanned arms to perfection. They were turning her on. She didn't remember the last time she had been around a man *this* good-looking.

God, his body was so *fine*. There wasn't a doubt in her mind that he worked out hard to keep his physique in tip-top shape.

His blue-gray eyes bored into hers and she wondered what he was thinking. Did he find her as attractive as she found him? Would he go out on a date with her if she asked? Taking a quick peek at his ring finger, she noticed it was bare.

When she called for a plumber she *never* thought she would get someone who would looked like him. He totally put all those other crack-showing plumbers to shame. How could he really be a plumber when his body was so perfectly made?

Whoa. She needed to calm down so she wouldn't stumble over her words. Ridge was hot enough to make any woman tongue tied.

"Okay, Ms. Falcon. Do you mind showing me where the toilet is so I can get it started?" Ridge broke into her thoughts, making Jaleena wonder how long she had been standing there gawking at him.

God, she hoped there wasn't a line of drool coming out of the side of her mouth. She resisted the urge to wipe it with her hand. It would be way too embarrassing if it came back damp.

"Jaleena will be fine," she corrected, then spun around. "Follow me. The toilet is right this way." Making sure not to look over her shoulder, she took Ridge towards the back of the store and the broken toilet.

Chapter Five

Setting his work bag down on the floor, Ridge stood over the toilet and looked at the food floating around in it. He wondered what exactly was going on with her and her brother. Whatever it was, there was a lot more to it than this stopped-up toilet.

"Does your brother always treat you like that?" he asked, looking at the pretty woman standing next to him. It had been such a long time since he had been around a female who made him stop working just to look at her.

Jaleena brushed a curl off her shoulder and avoided his direct stare. "Trent has a temper and sometimes it gets the best of him. I won't stand for him manhandling me. He better stay away from me, too, or I will call the police on him. His parole officer won't be happy if he gets into any more trouble. Trent is already walking a thin line with him as it is. "

Ridge wanted to say more, but he didn't feel like it was his place. He barely knew Jaleena and all he could think about was defending her. This had never happened to him before, and he wasn't sure how to handle it. Maybe it would be better if he stayed on the topic at hand, her toilet problem.

"Do you know what exactly he flushed down there?" Ridge asked. Bending down, he unzipped his bag and pulled out a plunger, drop cloth, and a couple of rags. Placing the drop cloth and rags around the toilet, he waited for her answer.

"It was a sandwich. He tossed it in there before I could stop him," Jaleena said, moving closer to him. "Do you think you can fix it? I can't have customers coming here tomorrow if I don't have a restroom for them to use."

"I won't leave until I get this fixed." Taking the plunger, he used it a couple of times and more food came up, but he could tell that he would have to do more because it was still stopped up. "Do you have a trashcan?"

"Yes, I do. I can go and get it for you."

While Jaleena searched the store for a trashcan for him to use, Ridge grabbed a pair of rubber gloves and pulled them on. A few minutes later, she came back in the room with a large black trashcan and placed it next to his bag.

"Thanks," he said. Reaching down, he grabbed the food and tossed it inside. "I think there is something else down there besides the sandwich Trent forced in there."

"Damn him," Jaleena cursed. "I can't believe he would do this to me. He knows how much time and not to mention money I put into tomorrow. I know he doesn't like the idea of *Talk of the Town*, but I didn't think he would attempt to sabotage me like this."

"Your brother doesn't seem like a very nice guy." Ridge made the comment as he was pulling the snake out of his bag. "Now, if anything is in there this plumber's snake will find it for you."

Inserting the snake into the toilet, Ridge gradually turned it as he inserted the spring into the drain. He kept moving it around until he felt something catch on the end of the hook. He slowly started to pull it out until the item came out of the toilet.

"Here's what started the problem." Grabbing the dirty washrag off the end, he showed it to Jaleena before he tossed it into the trashcan.

"I can't believe him! Why in the hell did he do that? I swear, if he shows his face here again I'm going to have him arrested. I'm not playing with him this time."

As Ridge began cleaning up the mess around him, he thought the same thing but kept his comments to himself. It wasn't his place to tell Jaleena what she should do with her life. Trent was still her brother. She might just be saying these things now because she was furious, but then change her mind later.

Standing up, he faced Jaleena and couldn't get over how stunning she truly was. There was just something about her that made him want to protect her. Despite the fact, she seemed quite capable of handling any situation that came her way.

He had been around black women before and had always found them very attractive, but this was the first time he thought of asking one out on a date. From past experience, he knew there were some black women who didn't date outside of their race. Back in high school, when he was on the football team, the black cheerleaders talked to him but they always went out with the popular black football players. Sure, when he was younger, he wasn't the best looking guy in the world. Yet, he knew how to play football and that helped him get a good spot on the team. He loved being a football player and benefited from the perks that went along with it.

However, his life changed after he decided to become a plumber. For some reason, he started working out more, drinking protein drinks, and added that much needed muscle to his slim frame. Women noticed the difference in him.

However, he didn't want any more overly tanned females constantly asking him out on dates. They were constantly asking him out: slipping their phone numbers in his hands, pockets, and anywhere they could place them. From the way they acted towards him, it was like he was an exotic male dancer at a bachelorette party or something.

Dragging himself from his past, Ridge looked down at Jaleena's lips and wondered how they would taste. *What would she do if I kissed her right now?* Did she sense the same attraction he did? Or was it all in his mind?

Chapter Six

"Ridge, are you okay?" Jaleena asked, touching him on the arm. She was having a hard time paying attention with him so close to her. The heat from his body made hers burn and wonder about things she shouldn't.

I wonder if he's single, she thought.

After taking another quick look at him, she shook that thought from her head and eased her hand away from his body. There was no way a man that damn hot was single.

"I'm okay. I'm just pissed your brother did this to you. Why would he want to sabotage you?" he asked.

"He has been like that ever since we were young. Sometimes, I forget that he's the oldest because I'm always taking care of him," she complained. "One day he will learn to stand on his own two feet, but enough about my brother. I want to thank you so much for fixing my problem. If you hadn't shown up, I don't know what I'd have done."

"I'm glad there was no real huge problem to fix," Ridge smiled. "You just have a little water cleanup that missed the protective covering I put down. Everything should go smoothly for you tomorrow."

Jaleena felt like a weight had been lifted off her shoulders. "I'm so happy to hear that. It took me six months to find this place. I loved it from the first moment I stepped inside."

"I wish you the best of luck with your business. I remember how nervous I was when I decided to open up my plumbing business with my Uncle Billy. It was a lot of hard work at first. I had to build up my client list, but it was worth all the sweat and tears." Reaching out, Ridge touched her on the shoulder and a light shock traveled through her body.

Jaleena didn't break eye contact with him. She wanted to see if he felt the same sizzling rush that she did. The shocked look on his face quickly answered her unspoken question. It had been years since she had been this drawn to a man without knowing anything about him.

She had always been level-headed when it came to the opposite sex. Still, she couldn't ignore how her heart raced and her palms sweat. Ridge stood so close to her, and all sorts of wicked fantasies were going through her mind.

Stop it now! she scolded herself.

She felt pretty certain that Ridge was attracted to her, but that didn't mean he would go the next step and ask her out on a date. She mentally told herself to move away before she humiliated herself and probably him, too.

"Hmmm…would you like a tour of the place before you leave?" Jaleena asked.

"I would love one," Ridge replied, removing his hand. She missed his touch immediately. "Let me clean this stuff up first."

"Great. I'll be in the front of the store waiting for you." Brushing past Ridge, she tried not to moan as the side of her breast brushed against his tanned arm. Lord, it wasn't right for one man to possess so much virility.

※

Ridge watched how well the jeans hugged Jaleena's ass as she moved past him into the other room. He had never been jealous of a piece of clothing until now. Jaleena was hot as hell and he wanted to ask her out to dinner and maybe a movie afterwards. She was just the type of woman he had been looking for. Jaleena was so different from Caitlin, in a good way.

Jaleena was strong and self-assured. He'd already figured that much from watching her deal with her brother and his issues. Yet, he could also tell that she had a fun and outgoing personality. He loved those qualities in a woman.

In the beginning of his on again, off again relationship with Caitlin, she pretended to have those qualities and he had admired her. Somehow, all of that changed when they started having sex—she quickly became jealous and controlling.

If he even smiled at the waitress taking their order, Caitlin would accuse him of sleeping with her. Her insecurities got old pretty quick and it was one of the main reasons he decided to end things between them.

It's a good thing I finally broke things off with Caitlin.

He didn't want anything or anyone standing in the way of him dating Jaleena, but he had to make sure she was interested in him first. He got the feeling that she was. Now, all he had to do was see if his intuition was right or wrong about what he sensed between them, because he wasn't about to assume anything.

Getting a dry rag out of his bag of supplies, Ridge

cleaned off the snake and placed it back into the bag along with everything else he had used to fix the toilet. He hurriedly cleaned up the little spots of water off the floor before tossing the rag in the trash can.

Washing his hands in the sink, Ridge dried them on a towel while thinking of a way to approach Jaleena to see if she would be interested in going out on a date. He couldn't waste any more time in the bathroom. Jaleena was waiting to show him around her business, and after they were finished he would suggest they go out to dinner. The worst thing she could tell him was no.

"Don't come on too strong. Flirt with her a little. Compliment her and then dive in to the good stuff. Ask her out." Ridge kept coaching himself as he picked up his bag and headed out the bathroom door.

God, I hope she doesn't turn me down.

CHAPTER SEVEN

Walking around the store with pride in her steps, Jaleena lovingly pointed out her favorite refurbished items to Ridge. She tried to block out how good he smelled. She always had a huge weakness for blue collar men, and Ridge most definitely fit the image she kept in her head. It was such a shame nothing would ever come out of her attraction to him. There was no way a man as fine as him wasn't married or in a committed relationship.

"Okay, I've bragged enough about my business," she said, making her way to the front of the store. "How much do I owe you?" Going behind the counter, she picked up her purse and took out her checkbook.

Ridge leaned across the counter, making her more nervous than she already was. Usually she was very confident when it came to men and knew how to flirt with them without a problem. He was throwing her off her game. She didn't know how to act around his raw masculinity.

"I hate to charge you for a problem that didn't take me fifteen minutes to fix," he answered. "How about you let me take you out to dinner tonight instead and we can call it even? Unless you have a boyfriend, or worse, a husband that I don't know about and he might come looking for me."

Jaleena knew her mouth had fallen open and she opened and closed it a couple of times before she finally had enough sense to just keep it shut. *Is Ridge reading my mind or something?* How else would he have known she was curious about him, too? *Lord...he is hot with a capital H.* She would be a fool to turn him down and her mama didn't raise no fool.

"I would love to have dinner with you," she said and smiled, shoving her checkbook back into her purse. "What time do you want to pick me up?"

She couldn't help but think about what she would wear, so she could get a second date with the hunk in front of her. She had a new black dress in her closet that she had been saving for a special occasion. Without a doubt, a date with Ridge would be more than extraordinary. He looked like he would know how to please a woman.

"I have to check with Uncle Billy and make sure he hasn't scheduled any more appointments for me. So, how about I pick you up in about two hours? Unless, you want to eat earlier and I can make the time to do what you want."

"Two hours will be perfect for me. I need to get a couple of more things done around here. How about I give you my phone number and address just in case you need to cancel?" First things first, she needed to call a locksmith to have her home locks changed, since Trent still had a key. She didn't want Trent to have access to her house anymore.

Reaching across the counter, Jaleena picked up one of her business cards and wrote her personal information on the back. She handed it to Ridge and watched as he slipped it into the back pocket of his well-fitting jeans.

"Oh, I'm not about to cancel on you. I've been thinking about a way to ask you out since I walked in here. I'm going to leave, but I will see you later." Ridge winked at her, picked up his bag off the floor, and left, leaving with her staring after him.

Chapter Eight

Jaleena didn't know how long she stood staring in shock at the door after Ridge's departure. Was she really going out on a date with a guy she just met? Sure, she had thought about dating a white guy before. She had never gotten the opportunity until now, and Ridge was sexy as hell. She wasn't about to turn him down.

God, her first crush had been on a boy named Mark Parker. His mother would have rummage sales that her mother would go to every Saturday. Of course, she would go just to see Mark. She had to have been around nine years old and he was about eleven.

Mark only lived in their neighborhood for about six months, but those months had been the best of her childhood. Mark and his mother were always so nice to her. They gave her a free Rice Krispies treat anytime they sold them, yet back then Mark was a kid and he was a part of her past. Ridge Taylor was a full grown man and thankfully here in the present. She wasn't about to miss out on this opportunity to get to know him better.

"Okay, I need to get everything closed up in here so I'll have enough time to get ready for my date."

Moving from behind the counter, Jaleena walked around her shop, making sure everything was in order. She was so wound up about tonight, but she wasn't about to leave her place of business in disarray.

Once she gave everything a good once over, she went back to the counter. Jaleena picked up her purse and was about to leave when her cell phone rang. Digging inside, she pulled it out, checked the Caller ID, and rolled her eyes. Shit, she didn't have time for this right now. Yet, she knew if she let the call go to voice mail he would keep calling back until he got a hold of her.

Flipping the cell phone open, she asked, "What do you want? Haven't you caused me enough problems today? Are you planning to come back for a repeat performance or something?"

"Little sis, is that any way to talk to your big brother?" Trent snapped back at her. "I was just calling to see if you thought about giving me the rest of the money I need. You know that you owe it to me. I mean, with all the good luck you have been having, it's only fair that you give some to me."

Had her brother lost his mind?

She wasn't about to give him any more money, especially after the way he treated her earlier. He better get that through his thick skull or he was going to be in for a rude awakening.

"I'm not giving you another penny," she tossed back. "How dare you call my phone asking for money after what you did to me?"

"I can call you anytime I want to."

"You better be glad Ridge was able to fix the toilet without too much trouble. When did you put the rag in there? You are just no good. You are like the bad seed or something. I can't believe we are even related."

"Ridge…are you talking about that pretty boy plumber? Why in the hell are you calling him by his first name? Never mind, I don't give a damn about his ass. I want that money and you're going to give it to me one way or another," Trent threatened.

Jaleena took several deep breaths and tried to calm down as she walked towards the front of the building. Trent knew how to push her buttons and she wasn't going to let him get away with it tonight. She had a date she was very thrilled about. Her brother wasn't about to ruin it for her with his idle threats. If he was in some kind of trouble, then he was going to have to get out of it without her help.

"Listen. For the last time, I'm not going to help you. You can harass me all you want, but it's not going to change anything, especially my mind. Goodbye." She abruptly disconnected the call and tossed the cell phone back into her purse. She turned off the lights and locked the door to her shop before making her way to her car and driving off.

CHAPTER NINE

"Did I tell you how good you smell tonight?" Ridge asked Jaleena as she placed the drink menu back down on the table. "I noticed it when you got inside my car and meant to tell you, but I don't know if I ever did."

"No, you didn't tell me, and thank you for the compliment," she said, smiling at him. "I'm glad you like it."

"Well, all I can tell you is that you're making it very hard for me to concentrate on food instead of you," he flirted again, making her feel good.

"I really must smell good because I heard this place is one of the best restaurants in town, and you're more focused on me than the food?" Jaleena grinned. She was so glad that she didn't talk herself out of this date. Ridge was really good company.

Crossing her legs, she leaned toward her date and stared into his gorgeous eyes. She couldn't believe how comfortable she felt around him. She wanted to get into his head a little more.

"I think you found out a lot about my life today because

of my brother. So, how about you tell me more about you?" she asked. "Are you an only child? Have you ever been married? Fill in the blanks for me."

Shrugging one of his broad shoulders, Ridge stared at her for a moment. "There really isn't much to tell. I'm the only child. When I was a kid my parents died in a plane crash, and after that horrible accident I went to live with my Uncle Billy and cousin Hank. Hank was only around a few months before he joined the Marines. After I graduated from college, I started the plumbing business with my uncle. He was the man you talked to on the phone earlier today. What else? Oh yeah, I have never been married and I don't have any kids."

"Oh, I'm so sorry to hear about your parents," Jaleena said. "My mother passed away several years ago and I still miss her terribly. She was my best friend in the world."

"Thank you," Ridge answered. "Have you and Trent always had such a bad relationship?"

"Trent has constantly wanted his way since we were little kids. I've tried my best to help him out, but today was the end. I'm done doing my sisterly duties when it comes to him. It's about time that he stands on his own two feet. Do you think I'm doing the right thing?"

"I don't know if you want my opinion or not," Ridge hedged.

Jaleena would love to hear what he had to say about this. Most of her friends thought she shouldn't give up on her brother because he was family and blood was thicker than water, but she was tired of his problems falling into her lap all of the time. He was the oldest. It was *way* past time that he started acting like it.

"Please tell me what you're thinking." She needed an

unbiased opinion about this because she was about to go crazy finding ways to deal.

"I believe in helping out your family. I wouldn't be here if my Uncle Billy hadn't helped me out. Still, I'm not into one family member taking advantage of the other one because he can. Your brother should have never put his hands on you this morning, and if that is his only way of handling things I think you need to get him out of your life and never look back."

Finally! Someone who sees the situation in the same light as I do, she thought.

"Thank you. I agree with you. I've done a lot for Trent, and you're right, it's time for him to be a man and handle his own responsibilities without involving me in them. He's going to be mad as hell, but he needs this and so do I."

"Enough about our families," Ridge said, reaching across the table.

He ran the tip of his index finger across the back of her hand. "I want to know how you are enjoying our date. I wasn't sure if you a vegetarian or not, but I love this steak house. The T-bone steak melts like butter in your month. I come here at least twice a year and just indulge in how excellent the food is."

Jaleena tried to pretend that Ridge's touch wasn't bothering her. God, she was dying to kiss him. That full bottom lip of his drove her crazy. Okay, she had to get her mind back on track here and keep her racing hormones in check. She wasn't some teenage girl on her first date with her crush.

"No, I eat meat. Sometimes, I don't think there's anything better in the world than a good T-bone steak with a side of hot French fries."

Winking at her, Ridge ran his finger across her hand

one last time before moving it. "You're my kind of woman. How about I get the waiter and we can order?"

"Sounds good to me," Jaleena answered, feeling excited about a date for the first time in years.

While she waited for Ridge to signal the waiter over to their table, she went over the day's events in her head. She never dreamt when she left the house this morning that she would be on a date with the hunk glancing over his menu. Ridge was amazing to be around. His charm was there, but it was so subtle that it was almost nonexistent. He was like the gorgeous man a woman saw across the room but didn't have enough courage to approach.

He was a far cry from the men Trent shoved at her since he got back home. Why in the world would she ever want to go out with any of the guys who landed him in prison for seven years? As far as she could tell, Ridge seemed like a very good guy and she was very interested in learning more about him. She secretly hoped there would be a second, third, and fourth date in their future.

"Are you okay?" Ridge asked her, making her focus on him and not her daydreams. "Your mind seemed like it was a thousand miles away."

"I'm fine." Jaleena couldn't think of a better word to describe tonight. "I was just wondering how soon I could ask you out on a second date."

Ridge was about to answer her when his cell phone rang and cut him off. He pulled it out of his jacket pocket and looked at her. "I'm sorry about this. I can let it go to voice mail."

"No, go ahead and see who it is. I don't mind at all."

Ridge wished that Jaleena had told him not to answer it because he knew who it was. It was same person who had called him five times before he left for this date tonight. *Why can't she get it through her head, it's over between us?* He didn't want to speak with Caitlin anymore, but he couldn't just let the phone keep ringing.

"Hello?" he answered.

"I thought you were going to call me," Caitlin told him. "I've been home all day waiting to hear from you. I wanted to finish our discussion from this morning. Did that plumbing problem turn into something bigger than you first thought?"

"Yes, it did. But, I got it taken care of," he replied. He didn't want to get into this, not with Jaleena sitting across from him. This was her time with him, not Caitlin's.

"Well, you couldn't have taken a moment to call me?" she whined in his ear. "I need to change your mind about us. I swear that I can stop trying to make you over into what I think you should be. I can let you be your own man if that is really what you want, but just don't end things between us. I really care about you a lot. I think we have a wonderful time together. How about I come over and we can find a way to work things out?" What Caitlin wanted was clear in her Southern-accented voice, but he was no longer interested in taking the bait. She wasn't going to get back into his life.

"I apologize for not calling. I don't think the second part of your suggestion is going to happen. I meant what I said earlier. I hope you understand nothing is going to change."

Ridge hated having this conversation with Jaleena right in front of him, but maybe it was for the best. Caitlin had to understand for once and all that he wasn't coming back to her. He felt something with Jaleena and he was going to explore it as much as it could. He would be crazy not to do it, and there wasn't a thing Caitlin would do about it.

"Fine," she snapped, and then rang off.

Shaking his head, Ridge closed his phone and shoved it back into his jacket pocket. "I'm sorry again about that. I shouldn't have taken that call. I swear it won't happen again."

"Let's not worry about it," Jaleena said. "I see the waiter coming. How about we order and enjoy the rest of our date?"

"I love the way your mind works," he answered a second before the waiter stopped beside their table and asked for their orders.

Chapter Ten

"I had a really good time tonight," Jaleena said as Ridge walked her back to her front door. "I can't remember the last time I had so much fun on a date just talking with a guy."

"I have to agree that you were a wonderful companion. I know you said it didn't matter, but I want to apologize again for taking that phone call at dinner. I shouldn't have answered it," Ridge said as he paused on her doorstep.

"I hope it didn't give you a bad impression of me, because I would love to have a second date with you. What do you say?" Moving closer to her, Ridge slid his hand behind her neck and eased her closer to his hard body.

The touch of his muscular chest against her breasts made her nipples harden instantly. Jaleena wondered how in the hell could Ridge wonder if she wanted a second date with him? Wasn't she the first one to bring it up on their date? Now the only thought in her mind was kissing him. Hell, she *never* kissed a guy on a first date, but Ridge would be the exception to her golden rule. She had to know what his lips felt like against hers.

"Hmmm…I'm not sure if I can agree to a second date or not," she whispered, sliding her arms around Ridge's neck. God, she was so forward with him, but she couldn't help it. He brought the bad girl that she never knew she had hid all of these years out of her.

"What do I have to do to coax a yes from those beautiful lips of yours?" he asked, pressing her body against his some more.

"I think a kiss might help me make a final decision." Jaleena heard the sensual sound of her voice and it even surprised her, so she could only imagine what Ridge was thinking. Was she being too assertive? At this moment, she honestly didn't care. She wanted a kiss from him and she was going to get it!

"It would be my pleasure, beautiful." Ridge's lips brushed against hers as he spoke.

The tip of his tongue explored the side of her mouth before slipping inside. Standing on her tiptoes allowed Jaleena get the full feel of Ridge's lips against hers. He moved his mouth over hers, as though learning its softness and taking control in a way no other man had ever done before.

The kiss made her body come alive with passion and a burning need to have more and more, but she couldn't. Now wasn't the time to drag this gorgeous man into her empty bed and let him have his way with her. They still needed to get to know each other better, but she could already tell she was going to have a hell of lot of fun doing it.

Ending the kiss, she took a couple of steps back. "We need to stop," she breathed past her swollen lips. "I didn't know it would go this far." Her mind relived the hotness of their first kiss as she tried to make her traitorous body listen to her reasonable mind.

Ridge moved his talented lips from her mouth down her neck, then over to her ear. Pulling it between his teeth, he nibbled at it for a couple of seconds before finally releasing it. "Damn, I hate that you're right. I would love to carry you inside and make love to you for the rest of the night, but I'll respect your wishes."

I'm such an idiot. Jaleena silently scolded herself as Ridge moved back until their bodies were no longer touching. *I should have lived in the moment and not pushed him away.*

"I better go before I change my mind and try to seduce my way into your house." He sighed, running his fingers through his thick brown hair. "Without a doubt, I'll be dreaming about you tonight, even after I take a much needed cold shower."

She couldn't believe what he just told her. A part of her was blown away by his open appreciation. Yet, another part of her didn't know what to say to him. How could she tell a man she just met that she felt the same wild connection with him, too? No, it was way too early for these kinds of emotions about Ridge. She knew nothing about him. First, she had to make the opening of *Talk of the Town* amazing, and then she could focus all her attention on building something with Ridge.

"You sure know how to make a woman feel special," she said, smiling. "I think I'm really going to love getting to know you better."

Stepping closer to her, Ridge ran his finger down the side of her cheek. "Does that mean my compliments along with my kisses will get me a second date for tomorrow? I know you have a lot going on tomorrow, but I would still love to take you out to a celebration dinner afterwards. Do you think you will be up to it, or should I make it for later on in the week?"

"Yes, I would like that," Jaleena answered immediately before she could change her mind.

"Are you sure that you're going to be okay?" he inquired. "I'm a little worried about leaving you here all alone after the fight you had with your brother. Will he come back and try to do something else to you?"

She was touched by his concern. Ridge was really a good guy. "No, I'll be fine. I had a locksmith come over here after work before our date, so I have new locks. Trent can't use his key to get in anymore."

An expression of satisfaction shined in Ridge's eyes as he pulled her into his arms. "I'll call you around six o'clock so we can finalize our plans." He gave her a soft kiss and then stepped back, waiting while she unlocked the front door. "Remember to stay out of trouble and not flirt with any men, or you might make me jealous." Turning on his heel, he went to his car, got inside, and drove off.

Standing on her porch, Jaleena went over the details of the day in her head. Ridge's confidence impressed her. A self-assured man was such a turn-on to her. Her body still vibrated from their kisses earlier, making her wish she hadn't let him leave. However, the waiting would give her more to look forward to later on, and waiting never hurt anyone.

CHAPTER ELEVEN

Throwing the phone across the room, Caitlin flung her body down on the bed as thoughts of Ridge filled her mind. Why hadn't he called her like he promised? Why did she have to end up calling him? He even sounded like she bothered him with her phone call. What was wrong with him lately?

He wasn't acting like the Ridge she had fallen in love with. What happened to the man who would make love to her all night long, so that the only thing she wanted to do the next day was lie in bed and recover?

It wasn't good for him to keep fighting his feelings for her. She already knew that he was in love with her. He was the perfect man for her. Why was he saying they were no longer a couple? It just didn't make any sense to her at all. She needed to take him on a trip so the two of them could talk about their future. She was beyond ready to be Mrs. Ridge Taylor.

If he worried about money he shouldn't, because she had enough for both of them. She could take care of them for the rest of their lives. Her husband's death left her a very wealthy woman, and she wanted to share her riches with only one man.

God, she had wasted her youth being married to Donald Alexander. She had been his live-in lover for several years before he finally decided to make their relationship legal. How was she supposed to know that after ten months of marriage he would die of a sudden heart attack, leaving her everything? Sometimes things just happened in life, and unfortunately Donald wasn't young enough or strong enough to keep up with her, but she wasn't going to blame herself for his untimely death.

She did love her husband when she first married him, but after a while Donald became insulting and very mean to her. She never told anyone how he would call her fat or stupid for no apparent reason. The verbal insults always came when she least expected them. All she could do was pray for his tongue lashings to end and they finally did. No, she couldn't say that she was sad that her husband was gone. It was past time she got some happiness back into her life, and Ridge would give it to her.

Ridge was the man she wanted. Caitlin wasn't going to let Ridge just throw her away. She would never forget the day she got up enough nerve and finally called the phone number.

Honestly, she wasn't having a problem with her kitchen sink, but she had to see if all the rumors about the sexy plumber in town were actually true. Her best friend Rita Simmons had told her about Ridge, but she had left out how unbelievably sexy he turned out to be.

She pursued him shamelessly, and two weeks later they were dating. Shit, Ridge had given her the best sex of her life. Her late husband thought he was an excellent lover, but his sexual abilities *never* made her see stars like Ridge's lovemaking did. He made her feel like her orgasms would last forever...

The sex between them was so out of this world that she offered to buy him a bigger place for his business. She didn't realize she had insulted him until Ridge climbed out of her bed and got dressed. He informed her that he wasn't interested in her wealth or what it could buy for him. In addition, he had warned her if she didn't stop trying to buy him things he was going to break up with her.

She was overjoyed he wasn't with her because of her wealth. She did learn some things after the time she spent with her husband, Donald. Everyone did have a price and all she had to do was find out how much Ridge was worth and then he would be hers.

Of course, she wasn't about to believe that Ridge had really broken up with her. He was only pissed because she offered to buy him a tuxedo for the mayor's party on New Year's. She should have approached him differently about it. How could she forget how sensitive he was about being thought of as a kept man, or "boy-toy," as he called them? All she had to do was find a way to get back on his good side and everything would be back the way it was....with him at her side and in her bed.

Getting out of bed, Caitlin picked up a cigarette off her nightstand and lit it. Taking a long puff, she blow out the smoke while thinking about a way to get herself back into Ridge's life. Well, first she would have to quit smoking. He hated the smell and how she tasted when they kissed. So, if she really wanted him in her life the cigarettes would have to go.

Walking around the room, she wondered who he had

been out with tonight. She wasn't dumb. She could tell from the way he talked to her on the phone that he was on a date with another woman.

Her man was good-looking. Women were bound to throw themselves at him, but she couldn't let him fall for one of them. Ridge was hers! She wasn't going to give him up, not now…not ever!

After several minutes, Caitlin finally pushed Ridge to the back of her mind and thought about her other problem. She was still pissed as hell because those dumb, high-priced movers lost her brand new three-thousand dollar-black divan.

Why in the hell did she let them move her furniture without her being there to supervise? It was her fault that it was now probably inside of someone's house. Thankfully, she had it insured and a new one would be here by the end of the week.

"Fuck, why am I thinking about a stupid divan? I need to focus on getting Ridge back," she said, taking another puff of her cigarette. He was the man in her life now, and it would stay that away for as long as she wanted it.

CHAPTER TWELVE

Two hours after her date with Ridge, Jaleena climbed out of the cast iron Marie Louise bathtub and enjoyed the smell of shea butter soap on her body. She was on her last bar, so she would definitely have to go out to Bath and Body Works and buy a few more.

Picking up the fluffy white towel off the sink, she wrapped it around her body. Her bathroom was done in all white and every time she came in here it gave her such a peaceful feeling.

Leaving the bathroom, she made her way back into her bedroom. Sitting down on the bed, Jaleena picked up the extra towel she left there. She still couldn't comprehend why Trent wanted to sabotage her new business and insult her the way he did.

How dare he imply that she didn't know how to spend money wisely?

He was just pissed that she hadn't squandered her money the way he had in less than six months. If he had picked better friends over the years, instead of the kind who wanted him to waste his half of the inheritance, he wouldn't be in whatever mess he was in now.

Trent thrived on getting attention from other people; it didn't matter if they were good or bad, as long as he was not left out in the cold. No matter how many times their mother told him to stop listening to other people and taking the wrong path, her brother blew off their mother's advice and did what he wanted to do because it felt good to him. He loved the instant gratification it gave him. He lived in the moment and never thought about planning for the future.

Why should he, when he just could bully people into doing what he wanted, not caring if he hurt their feelings or not?

Hell, she had even let him come and stay with her after he got out of jail because he was her brother. All her friends kept saying over and over, *You can't let your brother live on the street, he's family*. So, being the nice person she was, she let Trent move in her extra bedroom, but that was over now. All of his things were bagged up at the front door. Whenever he decided to make an appearance again, his things were ready and waiting for him.

It was sad she couldn't trust Trent, but he had done that to himself, not her. She had to think about herself first now, not him.

Jaleena finished drying off and put on her nightgown. She was tired and ready for bed, but she couldn't get Ridge out of her mind. "I can't believe how incredible my date was with him," she said out loud. "I don't know the last time a man made me feel so special. He actually listened instead of trying to talk over me. It was about me tonight instead of his problems."

She was dying to talk to him, but it was probably too late

to call him. Ridge was probably in bed asleep like she should be, but she was too excited about tomorrow. There was no way her body was going to let her get a good night's sleep.

If I was with Ridge right now I wouldn't be thinking about sleeping, either, she thought as she got up from the bed and turned back the covers. Without a doubt, they would find more pleasurable ways to pass the time until the early morning hours.

"Okay, I can't go down this road or I'll have to take a cold shower. Yes, Ridge does have a killer body. One that I wouldn't mind getting to know a little better," Jaleena said to herself as she crawled into bed. "However, that isn't going to happen tonight. So, I need to get my fantasies under control and get some sleep." Shoving her sexy thoughts about Ridge to the back of her mind, she reached to turn out her light at the same time the phone rang.

"Hello," she answered.

"What are you wearing?" a male voice asked.

Smiling, Jaleena snuggled further into the bed and pressed the phone against her ear at the deep, sexy sound of Ridge's voice. She was thrilled to hear from him. She decided to have a little fun with him.

"Sir, I don't know who you are. So, why would I answer that question?"

"I believe you know who I am," Ridge replied, lowering his voice. "I was the man who hated leaving you on your doorstep earlier tonight. I wanted to come in and make out with you on the couch like a couple of horny college kids, but I didn't."

An exotic image of her and Ridge popped into her mind, and Jaleena almost choked on her moan. Shit, she hated that he was such a gentleman. She could tell he was a bad boy and she was dying for that side of him to come out more.

"I wouldn't have stopped you," she admitted softly.

"Baby, you're playing with fire," he whispered. "Now, tell me what you're wearing so I can have something to dream about tonight. You honestly have no idea how lonely I am."

"I'm wearing pair of red bikini cut panties with a black heart imprint above my left butt cheek. They are very sexy." She wasn't really wearing that, but how would he know? This was supposed to be a game of seduction.

"Do they allow your ass to peek out a little?" He practically moaned the words into the phone.

"Of course, I wouldn't wear anything else."

Jaleena heard the sounds of sheets rustling around, and could only guess what Ridge was doing in his big, lonely bed. She already had him hot and bothered. What else could she do to make him lose control?

"Are you okay? Was it something that I said?" She hoped she was getting to him just like he was getting to her.

"Baby, you shouldn't tease me like this. I'm going to get you back if you don't stop," Ridge promised with a low rumble, sending tiny shockwaves all through her aroused body.

"Promises, promises," she sighed. "Guys have promised me things before and never lived up to my expectations. How can I be so sure that you will keep your word?"

"I'm not like the guys you have dated before. Sweetheart, when I make you a promise I will keep it," Ridge whispered in her ear.

Jaleena knew she had to change the subject or she would beg Ridge to come over and prove her wrong. "Well, I told you what I was wearing. How about you return the favor: boxers, briefs or, better yet, nothing at all?"

"Do you really want to know? It might be too much for your young heart to handle," he teased her.

"I'm positive that I can handle anything you have in that mind of yours to do to me. Now, are you going to tell me or will I have to come over there and find out for myself?" she asked in a low, silky voice.

Jaleena heard Ridge's full masculine laugh. "Darling, I know you aren't about to come over here, late as it is, so I'm going to keep what I wear to bed a surprise."

"Damn you," she tossed back, then giggled. "You sure do know how to ruin a girl's night. Here I thought we were going to have a little heated phone sex."

"I love phone sex like the next man, but I can't keep you up late. I know you have a very special day tomorrow."

Jaleena was touched that Ridge thought about her, though they had only been out on one date. Tomorrow was a crucial day for her. Sleep was important, but Ridge had her mind focused on other things. She would never get to sleep now. She was dying to know if he slept naked.

"Can't you tell me, please?" she begged.

"No, I'm going to let it simmer in the back of your mind until it drives you crazy with need. Goodnight, gorgeous," he whispered before hanging up on her.

"Oh, I can't believe he did that to me." Jaleena tossed the phone back on the stand next to her bed. "I swear I'm going to get him back for that," she promised as she snuggled underneath the covers and closed her eyes.

CHAPTER THIRTEEN

Standing in the back of *Talk of the Town*, Ridge watched as Jaleena interacted with an inquisitive customer wanting to know about an antique writing desk. He couldn't help but notice the pure pleasure on her face. He couldn't get over what an excellent time he experienced with her last night, and the only thing they had done was share a very hot kiss.

Absolutely no sex had been involved, and it only made him want her more, because he couldn't remember the last time he didn't get laid on a first date. Caitlin was always ready to give it to him every time they went out together, but he was looking for more fulfillment than an easy bed partner. He wanted to be stimulated, but in a different way.

Jaleena had a fun and cute side that was so contagious. He loved how they joked around on the phone last night. He had called her to say goodnight, but ended up having the time of his life. How could he not want to learn more about her? She was just the freshness his usual routine of working day end and day out needed.

The sound of a customer calling Jaleena's name made

him focus his attention back on the present, and the woman he saw as someone he could spend more and more time with. She was so engrossed in her work that she hadn't even noticed him in the store yet. He promised to come back and, being a man of his word, here he was.

In all of his adult life, he had never really been this instantly attracted to any woman, and he started dating at fifteen. Sure, Caitlin had been fun to be around when they initially started dating, but he never thought about her late at night or even while he was at work.

She only crossed his mind when she was right in his face, which wasn't how he would've wanted it. They were more like friends with benefits back then, and now their relationship was finally over. He didn't know what he had been missing until Jaleena came into his life.

She sparked a fire in him that he never knew existed. He had wanted to jump in front of her when her brother was yelling at her. God, he hated to think what would've happened to her if he had shown up only a few minutes later.

Now that she had him, he would make sure her brother understood the meaning of the word respect. *Whoa, what a minute.* What in the hell was he doing? Jaleena hadn't told him they were in a relationship. She might only want them to be friends and nothing else. He might be jumping the gun.

No! He wouldn't stand for being only friends with her. Jaleena was the woman he wanted. He would make damn sure he got his point across to her, loud and clear.

Leaning against the back wall, he slid his hands into the front pockets of his jeans and watched Jaleena as she worked the room. Anyone who watched him might think his relaxed pose made him seem like he didn't have a care in the world. In reality, he was plotting a way to make Jaleena a more important part of his life.

※

Jaleena worked on giving the correct change back to the woman in front of her, but she was having trouble not staring across the room at the man watching her. She had noticed Ridge the second he sauntered through the front door, drawing more than her attention, but she was too caught up with customers to acknowledge him.

Double damn. How could it be possible for a man to get better looking overnight? Today he wore a black T-shirt that resembled the one from yesterday. His jeans were snug in all of the right places. Just thinking about stripping them off his tall, muscular body made her mouth water. Lord, she had to get herself under control or she wouldn't be able to finish this final sale.

"Thank you for coming to *Talk of the Town*. Please come again," she said, handing the woman the correct change along with the receipt.

"I love it here," the woman replied. "It's so cute and the prices are so practical, especially with me being on a budget. I can come in here and find what I want without worrying about spending too much. I'm planning to come back tomorrow and bring my two sisters with me. They both love a good sale."

"Thank you. I hope to see you tomorrow." Jaleena waved at the woman as she opened the door and walked outside.

A sense of pride filled Jaleena as she came around the counter and noticed several sold stickers on the big ticket items in her shop. Without a doubt, she had made over two thousand dollars today with her grand opening, and things were only going to get better for her. It seemed like all of her dreams might be coming true after all.

Moving over to the door, she flipped the closed sign and locked the door. She had to do something so she wouldn't keep drooling over Ridge. He had actually shown up like he promised, and that showed her what kind of man he was. She wasn't fond of men who couldn't keep their word.

"Looks like you had a good day," a warm breath whispered by her ear.

Spinning around, Jaleena looked up into Ridge's warm gray eyes and was taken aback by the wonderful scent of his cologne. "Yes, I had an excellent day. My grand opening went better than I thought it would. I'm so pleased. Hopefully, the word will get around and more people will come tomorrow."

"Sorry, I wasn't here sooner. I had a couple of jobs that ran kind of late," Ridge apologized, then kissed her. "Can I make it up to you?" he asked against her moist mouth. "I would hate for you to be disappointed in me."

"What do you have in mind?" she inquired, running her hands over the front of Ridge's shirt. She loved the hint of muscles that she felt underneath. She was counting the days until she finally got to see them.

"How about you finish closing up the shop and I'll be more than happy to show you."

"Give me a few minutes and I'll be ready. I can't wait to see what you have planned for me."

The promise of something sexy hung in the air as Jaleena eased out of Ridge's arms and took care of last minute details so she could leave. She could only imagine what Ridge had in store for her.

She had never moved this fast with another man before

and, as much as she hated to admit, it was sort of fun living from moment to moment. Whatever Ridge was thinking about doing, she was more than ready for it.

CHAPTER FOURTEEN

"I can't believe how good that feels," Jaleena moaned as she leaned back on the divan. "I don't know how I made it this long without you and those magical hands."

"I'm always here to please you," Ridge chuckled as his fingers worked their way up her calf. "Call me anytime you want this done. I love any time I get to touch your pretty body."

Opening her eyes, Jaleena glanced at her legs draped across Ridge's hard thighs as he massaged her tired feet. It was a feeling out of this world after being on her feet for close to eight hours today. After they left *Talk of the Town*, Ridge took her out to dinner then brought her back to his place and surprised her with the foot massage.

"How did you know I would be so hungry?" she asked, getting more comfortable on the cushions. "I never eat that much."

"I noticed how late it was when I got to your store and I knew you had to be starving. So, I wanted to treat you a nice, quiet dinner. Did you like it?" he asked, moving his hands from her left foot over to the right one.

"Couldn't you tell how much I loved it by how quickly I gobbled everything down?" she replied, slightly embarrassed.

"Don't be ashamed. I love a woman that knows how to enjoy a meal. Watching you eat was turning me on," he confessed as his hand slid up her leg. "I hope you show that kind of passion when it comes to other things."

"What other things do you have in mind?" Jaleena asked, moving her legs off Ridge's hard thighs.

"Are you sure that you're ready for this?" Ridge asked, lifting her off the divan and straddling her body over his legs. "I don't want to rush you into anything. We haven't known each other that long."

Jaleena ran her fingers through Ridge's thick brown hair. Why was he asking her this? She didn't want to be any other place. Everything just felt so right when it came to him. He wasn't forcing her to do anything she wasn't ready for, but she wanted to make love with him.

"I've never been more positive about anything in my life," she answered, hoping that he lived up to her fantasy where so many other men had failed.

"God, I was hoping you would say that," he confessed, getting up from the divan and taking her with him. "I've wanted to see this beautiful body of yours naked since the first I laid eyes on you."

"That's so good to hear," Jaleena said as she wrapped her legs around Ridge's waist. "I have been dying to see your sexy ass naked, too."

"Ms. Falcon, I aim to please." Walking the short distance to his bedroom, Ridge tossed her down on the bed and stared into her eyes. All she could think about was him making this a night she would never forget.

CHAPTER FIFTEEN

Relaxing in the middle of the bed, Jaleena watched as Ridge moved over to the bedroom door. "I don't want anyone interrupting us," he said as the lock clicked loudly in the room.

"Do you get a lot of visitors?" she inquired, kicking off her shoes.

"Sometimes my Uncle Billy comes over to check on me, and I would hate for him to walk in on us." Moving towards her, he eyed her body like she was a present he was dying to unwrap. He wanted to find out what was hiding inside the pretty wrapped box.

"When am I going to get to meet this uncle of yours? You mentioned him before, so he must be an important part of your life."

"Baby, I love my uncle," Ridge answered, leaning over her on the bed. "But, I don't want to talk about him right now."

Tilting her head to the side, she arched an eyebrow. "Mr. Taylor, do you care to tell me what might want to do instead? I'm sure that you have plenty of ideas."

A devilish glint came into his eyes as he stared down at her. "I want to run my hands all over this gorgeous body of yours. Do you think you will be able to handle that? I have this wonderful scented coconut oil that I'm sure will smell so good on your skin."

"Oh, I adore the smell of coconut oil. I use it in my hair all the time," Jaleena replied. "What do you do with it?"

Ridge wasn't going to make Jaleena force him into saying the words. She knew why he had the oil and what he used it for. He bought a bottle of it the same night after his date with her because it reminded him of her unique scent.

"How about we stop talking and get down to business?" Sitting up on the bed, Ridge pulled her body up so they were eye to eye.

Grinning, she ran a finger across his full bottom lip and giggled when the tip of his tongue licked it. "Did I tell you how much I love a man that knows how to take charge?"

Ridge's left eyebrow raised a fraction at her comment before a smile pulled at his firm mouth. "I'll keep that little confession of yours in mind. Do you know how I'm dying to feel your smooth skin beneath my hands?"

Starting with the top button of her shirt, he slowly undid it while moving his hand slowly downward, making sure that the back of his knuckles brushed her heated flesh as they went. Slipping the shirt off her shoulders, he tossed it behind him and then cupped her breasts in the palms of his hands.

The pads of his thumbs brushed over the nipples, sending a pool of moisture to her panties. God, this man was too damn sexy for his own good. Even his thumbs were turning her on.

Was she some kind of kinky sex freak or something, and never knew it until now?

"Hmmm...that feels so wonderful," she purred in the back of her throat.

"Darling, it's only going to get better," he promised a second before his mouth lowered and replaced his thumbs. He slowly flicked his tongue back and forth over her hard nipple and then sucked on hard peak into his warm, wet mouth.

Slipping her fingers through the cool strands of his hair, Jaleena succumbed to the forceful domination of his lips on her body. It was like nothing she had ever felt before: hot, earth-shattering bliss. Emotions swirled through her limbs as she fell back on the bed, taking Ridge with her.

She whimpered underneath his hard body while his tongue swirled over her nipples, driving her wild with the need to have more...and more.

"Oh, yes." Jaleena gasped as the sensation of having Ridge's mouth on her body took over. "Ridge, *please....*" She pushed at his shoulders, hoping he would get the hint and give her what her body craved.

Leaving her breasts, he trailed a line of tantalizing kisses down her skin until he reached her belly button. He licked it a couple of times before he gave his complete attention to undoing her jeans.

Ridge quickly got rid of them, but he took his time removing her skimpy underwear. Grabbing the sides, he eased them down over her hips and her legs, then tossed them over his shoulder. A forefinger slid over her pussy before working its way inside and going deep.

The feel of his finger in her body had her crying out in pleasure. Slowly, he added another finger to tease her already aroused body. She couldn't take much more, it felt... Jaleena wrapped her hand around his thick wrist, trying to regain some sort of control.

"Do you know how truly beautiful you are?" he asked as his desire-filled gaze moved over her body inch by inch. His thumb brushed over her clit, making her hips rise off the mattress before moving back down.

"I'm alright," Jaleena stammered when she finally regained her voice. She was so taken aback by the look in his eyes that it left her momentarily speechless.

"You are more than all right, and I'm going to prove it to you tonight for as long as you need it," Ridge replied as he removed his fingers and then tugged his T-shirt over his head.

"Your body is amazing!" The words were out of her mouth before she could stop them. He was truly magnificent to look at, but why wouldn't he be? He was mouth-watering with his clothes on, so why wouldn't he make her speechless with them coming off?

Her gaze wandered over the dusting of hair on Ridge's toned chest that led down his six-pack to the noticeable, large bulge in the front of his jeans. There wasn't an ounce of fat on his waist. He had muscles in places that she never imagined possible.

"Thanks, babe, I'm glad you like what you see." Ridge worked on removing his shoes while she continued to get her fill of his perfect body.

She really must be horny if the act of Ridge taking off his work boots was turning her on. She was more than ready to get to know him in every sense of the word.

The moonlight coming through the bedroom windows highlighted his body perfectly, making her silently pray for

Ridge to touch her again. "Why are you standing there?" she whispered. "Why don't you come back over here? I'm getting lonely without you."

A dangerous glint came into his eyes as a masculine grin tugged at the corner of his firm lips. "Roll over on your stomach and lay perfectly still."

It sounded more like a demand instead of a request. Jaleena almost thought about not doing it, but at the last minute flipped over like Ridge instructed her to do for him.

The sound of a drawer opening behind her temporarily drew her attention making her wonder what in the world he was doing. She tried taking a peek over her shoulder to see what Ridge was doing, but he smacked her on the ass, shocking the hell out of her.

Chapter Sixteen

"Ouch, that hurt!" she cried out, not admitting how much the sting from the tap turned her on.

"Stop trying to sneak a peek or you'll get the same thing again," Ridge cautioned in a low, dangerously sexy voice.

"You wouldn't dare," Jaleena said, then looked over her shoulder again and got a second harder slap, this time for not listening to his warning.

"Hey…" she whined.

"I told you that I would do it again. Listen to what I tell you, woman, unless you like being smacked on the ass. Are you into kinky stuff?"

"No, I'm not into anything kinky," Jaleena denied, but a part of her did wonder about what sort of wild stuff Ridge might be into.

"Too bad," Ridge sighed behind her. "I want to show you something, but I guess now I can't." The bed dipped as he put his weight on it, and a few seconds later his hands touched the middle of her back and the scent of coconut drifted towards her nose.

"Oh, your hands feel so amazing."

"Just keep still and enjoy getting pampered."

Starting high on her back, Ridge moved his left hand counter clockwise and his right hand clockwise, and the movement slowly started to relax the tension in her back. After a few rubs on her back with the coconut oil, Jaleena got lost in the sensation of Ridge's talented fingers working her body. Little by little his strokes got bigger and bigger until he reached her nape. Jaleena's body was melting under Ridge's touch and she loved every second of it.

"Do you know how good this feels?" She moaned out loud. This was a dream come true. She always wanted a hot man to give her a massage, and she was finally getting it to happen.

Lord, Ridge was going to have her totally into him before the night was over, and there wasn't a thing that she could do to stop it.

"If I didn't, I do now from the sound of your moans," he breathed by her ear as his hands slipped down and massaged her butt.

"Keep on that track and I can promise you that my sighs of pleasure will get louder later," she promised him.

"Oh, I haven't thought about stopping for a second," Ridge told her. "I'll try to see what I can do." His hands moved as he worked on the legs. "Do you know how sexy your legs are? I couldn't stop looking at them the day of your opening. I was imagining how they would feel wrapped around me as we made love."

"Ridge Taylor, you are a bad boy," she moaned. "What am I supposed to say to that?"

"Have you have thought what it would be like if we made love, too?"

"Oh, I have. More times than I care to admit," Jaleena confessed.

"I think it's time for you to turn over. I want to look at the front of you. I know it's just as perfect as the back."

"Are you sure about that?"

"How could anything on this beautiful body of yours be an imperfection?" Ridge asked, then ran his hand down the middle of her back. "Now turn over, woman, so I can finish your massage."

Flipping over, Jaleena gasped when her eyes spied Ridge's cock. It was at least eight inches long and thick. There was a little bit of moisture at the end and she couldn't wait until it was inside of her. Hell, he could forget all about finishing the massage and just make love to her. She reached out to touch him, but he brushed her hand away. "No, you can't touch me. I wouldn't be able to last if you did."

"Can I touch you later?" she pouted as she dropped her hand back down on the bed.

"Babe, you can touch me all you want later, but only after I get to pleasure you." Ridge's words made her warm body even hotter.

Lifting her body off the bed, he slid it towards the edge and placed her left foot in the center of his chest. With his well-oiled hands, Ridge massaged the back of her calf and stopped a little bit above her knee. Usually she was really ticklish when it came to the back her knees, but he was turning her on too much to even notice.

"Your hands should be outlawed," Jaleena panted as he replaced her left leg with her right on his chest. He showed her new leg the same kind of exotic treatment.

"You know that I only do this for very special women." Ridge dropped her leg and knelt between her spread thighs.

She watched as he grabbed more of the oil, poured it into his hands, and rubbed them together to make the liquid warm.

"How many women have been graced with your massage skills?" she asked, a hint of jealousy in her voice.

He laid his hands on her thighs and slowly worked the oil into her legs. Ridge acted like he didn't hear her question, but she knew that he did. It wasn't like she whispered it or anything.

"You are the first and only," he answered as his fingers came close to her wetness, but he backed away without actually touching it. "I have never thought about doing something like this until now."

"I'm glad to hear that," she confessed. "I would hate to be another notch on your massage bed."

"You will never be a notch on my anything," Ridge told her as his fingers massaged the muscles in her stomach and inched their way up to her breasts. He played with her nipples before leaning over and drawing one into his wet, hot mouth.

"Shit, that feels so good," Jaleena moaned as she lifted her body off the bed.

She held Ridge's head to her breasts so he would suck harder. He got a little rough, nibbling and tugging at her hard nipples and causing her to scream his name.

"Bite me harder," she cried, pulling at the ends of his hair as hot sensations took over her body. Ridge listened to her and nibbled harder at her breasts.

"Oh, yes," she mewled, softly. She was so lost in the moment that she didn't flinch when Ridge thrust three of his coconut-oiled fingers inside of her body. She only bucked her hips faster to match the movement thrust of his fingers.

The orgasm hit her so hard and fast that Jaleena thought

she might pass out from it. God, she had never come with a man only using his fingers before. She didn't even think it was possible.

"Are you okay?" Ridge asked as he released her nipple and licked the side of her neck. "I didn't mean for that to happen. I wanted to be inside of you when you came for me the first time."

"You were inside of me," Jaleena giggled.

"You know that isn't what I meant," he growled, taking a nip at her neck.

"Well, if you're still up to it, I'm more than ready to do it again." She couldn't wait until she felt him buried deep inside her body.

"Oh, I'm willing and able." Getting off her body, she watched as Ridge pulled a condom out of the drawer next to his bed and put it on. He quickly covered her limbs with his body before she could really miss him.

CHAPTER SEVENTEEN

"You are so damn beautiful," Ridge whispered as he slid into her. He was halfway inside of her pussy. He slid back out then rocked his hips forward, thrusting deep inside her body. He linked their hands together and held them down on either side of her head, looking into her eyes as his body moved in and out of hers.

"Your pussy is so fucking tight and wet."

"Mmmm," she whimpered, rocking her hips in the same rhythm as his.

Jaleena watched Ridge's light gray eyes grow darker as she wrapped her legs around his waist. She couldn't remember ever being this close to someone before. There was something different about the way Ridge loved her. It was more intense, and fulfilling.

Her lips parted in a breathless, silent moan. His cock felt so good, she became helpless and lost in a daze of sexual fog burning with hot, tempting, mind blowing pleasure.

Dropping his head, Ridge slowly caressed her sensitive swollen nipples with his tongue. Letting go of her, his hand burnt a path down her stomach to her leg, which wrapped more securely around his waist as his thrusts became harder and deeper.

Grunting, Ridge buried himself balls deep inside of her pussy. She gasped as she grabbed onto the sheets.

"Oh, Ridge, your cock is so thick and hard," she moaned.

His bedroom filled with their panting and groans of pleasure, and he began speeding up his powerful thrusts. Jaleena loved the sound of his body brushing over her damp skin. Electric sparks tingled as they made their way through her body.

Suddenly, Ridge pulled out, then worked his hips and shoved his cock completely back into her tight pussy. He repeated the same movement over and over. Each time his dick went inside her, Jaleena realized that she never wanted another man inside of her again. His thrusts were powerful and on the mark. He knew how to make love to a woman and she was so damn glad to be on the receiving end.

She felt like a puppet in his masterful hands, but in a good way. A very good way!

He pressed his mouth against the shell of her ear. "Do you know how delicious you feel wrapped around my dick? I swear I don't want to be anywhere but inside of you for the rest of the night."

Ridge ran his tongue along the side of her neck before kissing his way down her body, and ended back at her breasts. He recaptured one of them, drawing it back into his mouth. He sucked it, rolling around the hard peak inside of his mouth and driving her crazy until she almost couldn't think straight.

Jaleena closed her eyes, pulling at the sheets beneath

her with her free hand. Lord, she was going to die from pleasure tonight and she didn't give a damn. Ridge hit her spot with his short, urgent strokes in ways she didn't believe possible until now. In the past, she was used to only long, deep ones but his were better...so much better. She couldn't get enough of them. The end of his penis hit her spot over and over. She knew her orgasm was coming.

"Come for me, baby," he whispered in her ear. "Let me see how stunning you look when you are coming apart in my arms."

When did his mouth let go of her nipple? Jaleena wondered. Had she been so lost in the moment, she hadn't even felt it?

"YES!" she screamed loudly inside the room, not caring she was letting herself go.

"That's it, baby," he encouraged, planting hot kisses all over her heated skin. "Tell me what you want. Let go for me. Give it to me."

"Please."

"Please what, Jaleena?" Ridge asked, placing his hands on her hips to hold her in place while he had his way with her. He slowed his movements until it felt like wasn't moving at all. "Is this what you want? Slow and easy," he panted. "I can give it to you."

"No," Jaleena whimpered, opening her eyes to reconnect her gaze with Ridge's heated look. "I want it like you were doing before."

A purely masculine grin pulled at the corners of Ridge's mouth as he worked his strokes harder and faster until it felt like her eyes would roll in the back of her head.

Her orgasm hit her out of nowhere. She screamed and clawed at Ridge's back as it ricocheted through her body, leaving her panting with her chest heaving. Ridge groaned loudly, twitching his hips as his own release took over. It seemed like his cock kept jerking inside over her again and again until his body gave out and he collapsed on her.

She didn't know how long she laid there beneath him, trying to regain control of her senses before she started squirming beneath Ridge's weight.

"Ridge, you're getting heavy," she complained.

"I'm sorry, sweetheart," he apologized as he rolled off her and tossed the condom in the trashcan by side of the bed. He pulled her flush against his body. "I can't believe I just experienced that. It was totally…"

She knew what Ridge was trying to say, but there were no words for it. She was just as blown away as he was by what happened between them. She didn't know a man was able to bring her so close to multiple orgasms before, but Ridge was about to until her body gave up.

"I know. I feel the same way," she confessed, more content than she had been in a very long time. "How about we get some sleep and see if we can do it even better next time?"

"You think it can get better?" he teased, running his fingers over her stomach.

"I'm a firm believer in being the best you can. What about you? Are you game, Mr. Taylor?"

"I think I'm going to like trying to be my best with you," Ridge answered as he covered them with a sheet and planted a soft kiss on her mouth. "Let's get some sleep so we can get up later and see what else we can do to move up that scale."

Chapter Eighteen

Folding his arms behind his head, Ridge relaxed in the middle of his rumpled bed as thoughts of Jaleena swirled around in his mind. She had left over twenty minutes ago, and he was still disappointed that he couldn't talk her into spending the night at his place...hell, in his bed.

The bed felt so empty and cold without her warm curves curled up next to him. He would have gotten up tomorrow morning and fixed both of them breakfast, something he had never done for Caitlin.

Most of the time he wanted a woman out of his bed soon after the lovemaking was over, but he didn't have that reaction with her. He wanted to wake up in the middle of the night and watch her sleep. He had tried several ways to make her stay with him, but in the end she had turned him down and left. She gave him some flimsy excuse about not wanting to run late for work tomorrow, but he knew that wasn't the true reason.

Jaleena was frightened of what happened between the two of them tonight. He had never experienced such closeness with a woman before. He wasn't a virgin by far, and never had claimed to be one.

Jaleena was the only woman to whom he had ever given the option of spending the night in his arms, and she turned him down. Hell, he *never* thought about allowing Caitlin a chance to get cozy in his bedroom for long, or he wouldn't have ever found a way to get rid of her.

Removing one of his hands from behind his head, he ran it across the light covering of hair on his chest. He inhaled the wonderful scent of Jaleena that still lingered in his bed. He wondered what was next for them. He thought… no knew, they would make the perfect couple. She was the independent woman he had been searching for. It didn't hurt that she could keep up with him in bed, too. That one special addition only made her hotter in his opinion.

Hell, he was a grown man now.

Past the age of wanting a causal relationship or a roll in hay with a tight, available body, he wanted Jaleena because she fit him and everything he desired in his life. He wasn't going to let her ease away from him. They had and could have more than wonderful sex going on between the two of them. No, now that he found her he wasn't about to allow Jaleena to do a vanishing act on him.

She might be a little nervous, but he would take his time and work through her concerns. It didn't matter how long it took, as long as she didn't try to avoid him after tonight. He wouldn't stand for it.

Jaleena Falcon ignited a fire within him the second he spotted her arguing with her brother at *Talk of the Town*. She had been scared and in pain, but she didn't allow Trent to see the agony she was really in at that moment.

He should have run across the room and pulled him

away from Jaleena. If he got another chance, Jaleena's brother was going to learn how to treat a woman with some respect, especially someone one as unique as her.

He gained more respect for Jaleena when she didn't flirt with him as soon as they were alone. Sometimes women clients did, and they would gossip about him and then find some oddball reasons for him to come to their houses. Half the time nothing needed to be fixed—wasted trips on his part.

A lot of lonely housewives in this town thought his services involved taking care of more than their house problems. It was funny sometimes, the excuses women would come up with to get him into their bedrooms. He would just tell them no and leave, and if they called again he would send Billy in his place. This usually stopped a third phone call from happening. His uncle laughed about the numerous fake calls when it first started to occur, but after a while it got on his nerves, too.

Now, when Billy got a hint that a plumbing call wasn't on the up and up, he would go first to check it out. If it turned out to be something real, his uncle would call him over to check it out for himself. The new way they set up to deal with the crank calls seemed to have stopped them for a while, and he was overjoyed about it.

Jaleena wasn't the type to play games like that, but if she was he wouldn't mind getting seduced in her bedroom... maybe he would find a way they could end up taking a shower together. Just the idea of being all soapy and wet in her shower had his cock leaping to life, and a moan escaped from his mouth.

"God, why did I let my mind go down that road? I knew where it would lead, and now Jaleena isn't here to help me with this problem."

Tossing the covers off his aroused body, he climbed out of bed and proceeded into the bathroom. A cold shower was in his future. If Ridge had his way tomorrow night, he wouldn't be taking one without help, because Jaleena's sizzling little body was going to be in there with him.

Chapter Nineteen

"Surprise."

"What are you doing here?" Jaleena asked, shocked and staring at the man on her doorstep. "I wasn't expecting you this early. I thought we decided to meet up later on since you had a job to take care of across town."

"Are you not happy to see me?" Ridge asked, smiling down at her. "I mean, you called me early this morning to help with the store and now you want to kick me to the side until you need my hands again. I guess I better leave and find another woman who will appreciate my talents better."

"No. I'm so glad that you came by," Jaleena whispered, wrapping her arms around Ridge's neck. "I just thought we weren't going to see each other until later on tonight since Billy needed your help. I had this romantic dinner planned, along with some other fun stuff for us to do."

"I tried to stay away, but I couldn't. I had to see you," he said, circling his arms around her waist. "How could I stay away after the night we spent together? I was thinking maybe we should do that full body massage again. I really like that. Who knows, maybe next time you could give me one?"

"Hmmm...that doesn't sound too bad to me. I guess I do need to give you a special treat for helping me pass out all of those flyers about the divan sale. That was so sweet of you. My surprise find is a very expensive item. I know that it will bring in a lot of money if I can sell it for the listed price."

"You are more than welcome," Ridge said, tugging her closer to his body. "I love helping out a stunning woman. I don't want a back rub, but I think that I should get something else."

"So, instead of a back rub, what should I give you as a thank you?" she asked. "I thought it would be something for both of us to enjoy."

Ridge shook his head. "No, I don't think that is going to work. I want something different, something better."

"Well, do you want me to fix you a home cooked meal? I'm a pretty good cook. We could go back to my house. I could fix up something to eat instead of you taking us out to dinner. We could eat in front of the fireplace. Its sounds like a very romantic idea to me."

"Jaleena, I bet you can cook the hell out of anything your little hand touches, but that isn't what I want. I'll give you one more guess."

"God, I don't have a clue," she teased, tracing Ridge's bottom lip with her finger. "I thought all of my ideas were good. You might have to help me out here. Give me a hint or something. I'm sure that I'll be able to figure it out after that."

"You need a hint from me?" His tongue darted out and licked the end of her finger. "I don't know if I'm up to giving out hints or not. I know we haven't been together that long, but I think you should be able to read me by now. What do you think I *really* want from you?"

Jaleena tilted her head to the left and then to the right. She knew that Ridge wanted her to kiss him, but she was having so much fun messing with him, pretending that she didn't. She wondered how long she could keep this going on before he figured out she was teasing him.

"I got it." She grinned. "You want me to help you on your next plumbing job. I don't know anything about fixing a stopped up drain, but I can hand you all of the correct tools."

"Jaleena, stop teasing me and kiss me," he growled as his mouth lowered slowly towards hers.

"I thought you would never ask," she said a second before his mouth claimed hers.

She kissed Ridge back, savoring every moment of their time together. She loved how her body melted against his like they were trying to fill a hunger that neither one truly wanted fulfilled anytime soon. It was more fun working towards the end goal instead of completing it.

Parting her lips, she raised herself on her tiptoes so Ridge could deepen the kiss. It didn't take a second coaxing from her before he eased his tongue inside of her mouth. Without saying a word, she brushed her body against his, telling Ridge with body language what she wanted.

Ridge swept her up into his arms and carried her from her living room into her bedroom. She didn't doubt that she was in for a very special night, because the last time she made love to Ridge it left her breathless. So, there was no telling what a repeat performance was going to do to her. She was just glad she took her vitamins this morning.

Chapter Twenty

Staring at the flyer in her hand, Caitlin turned it over a couple of times to make sure she wasn't seeing things, but she knew she wasn't. The proof was right there in front of her eyes. She had come to get her nails done and found this lying on the table by her favorite magazine.

Who in the hell had laid this here?

How could this be possible? Someone was trying to sell her black divan at a thrift store. How in the fuck had this person gotten their hands on her expensive property? Had those stupid drivers not really lost her divan, but given it to this Jaleena Falcon woman instead?

Were they in this together? Was she really a thief pretending to be a store owner?

Well, she was going to get down to the bottom of this right now. She wasn't about to be made a fool by anyone. She was going to get her property back and have this woman tossed in jail. Ms. Falcon was about to find out what happened when she messed with someone who had power, money, and influence in this community.

She hadn't reported it missing because she was too embarrassed that she let her neighbor and his friend move the furniture for her. Now she was going to do everything in her power to make sure all of them got what they had coming to them for lying to her like this.

Getting off the couch, Caitlin snatched up her purse and stormed out of the hair salon. With the flyer in her hand, she got inside her car and sped off to take care of the problem before somebody bought her divan from this store. She would never step foot inside a used furniture store, but today she was going to do it. She hated when people didn't know how to work for the things they wanted and instead stole from others.

She worked hard in that hellish marriage of hers and everything she bought with her deceased husband's money was hers! She wasn't about to let anyone take it from her, let alone some greedy bitch trying to make a quick buck off her back.

"I'm going to make sure that this woman learns her lesson about taking something that isn't hers," Caitlin said to herself as she headed for *Talk of The Town*.

On the drive, Caitlin let her mind travel to Ridge and what happened between the two of them. What in the hell was wrong with him? Hadn't she been good to him since they first started sleeping together? She never looked down on him because he was only a plumber. Most of her girlfriends told her how they tried to get him into their beds, but he turned them down.

They didn't understand Ridge wasn't going to crawl between the sheets with them for any price. He actually thought he was worth something because of that run-down plumbing business of his. God, he didn't understand that he would never be in the same circle or class as the men she knew.

Sure, he made an excellent arm accessory when she needed a date. She wasn't about to deny that he could work her body like no other man ever had in her forty-plus years, but that was all he would ever be worth.

Ridge Taylor, with his closet full of t-shirts and well-worn jeans, wouldn't know how to clean up nicely if his life depended on it. That was the one reason she supplied him with suits when they went out to important social events. He wouldn't even know where to go to have a suit custom made for him.

She couldn't have him embarrassing her by showing up dressed inappropriately. She loved doing things for Ridge; yet, he resented her and she never understood why. Most men would love to be schooled by an older, more experienced woman. Ridge fought her tooth and nail about everything.

God, he was the best lover she'd ever had. Not like her dead husband, who only liked really rough sex and tried to get it every night. Most of the time she let him do it so he would just shut up and leave her alone.

However, Ridge wasn't like that at all. He made her feel special each and every time they made love at her house. Only twice did she have sex with Ridge in his own bed, and it hurt deeply that he made her leave, but she chalked it up to him still living with that old man, Billy, back before he moved out and got his own place.

He constantly had excuses about not wanting him to walk in on them. Well, if he would finally put that old man in a nursing home where he belonged, she could spend the night there more often. It would be even better if she could get Ridge to sell the house and move into her place, which had more rooms that she would ever use in this lifetime.

If Ridge would get over whatever was bothering him, she might be interested in making him her next husband. There was no doubt in her mind that the two of them would get along perfectly in the bedroom and it would pour out into the other aspects of their lives.

Yet, he thought that sex was the only thing she truly wanted from him. This wasn't far from the truth; however, she did have other plans for him. None of them were so bad that Ridge wouldn't agree to any of them.

First, he would have to sell that stupid ass plumbing business of his. There would be no reason for him to work, given her wealth. They could spend all their time together and maybe take a trip or two.

Finally arriving at her destination, Caitlin turned off her car and got out. She stood by the side of her car and looked around. She hated areas like this. They were always an unwelcome reminder of her past. The poor always used stupid get rich quick schemes to trick some unaware person out of his money. Just being here made her skin crawl and, for a split second, she thought about just leaving it alone and going home. But, the idea of some lowlife making money off her things turned her stomach, and she would make sure it wouldn't happen.

Brushing her hair off her shoulders, Caitlin fixed her clothes and headed for the front door of *Talk of the Town*. "I'm going to show this Jaleena Falcon that she doesn't mess with me or my stuff. After I finish with her, she is going to wish she never stole my divan."

"How dare she let him talk to me that way!" Trent complained. "Jaleena is my sister and she should have stood up for me. Hell, we fight all of the time, but isn't that what siblings are supposed to do?"

Trent sat in the shady Yellow Rose Bar and Grill. It was his favorite place to come and think. None of his friends knew about it, and Jaleena sure as hell wasn't aware of it. She would give him a lecture about being here. She would be even more pissed to know this is where he had wasted most of his money after their mother died.

He had hung out in this particular bar before he got sent off to jail. Hell, everyone here was the same and no one looked down on others. His friends here agreed that he needed a break, but was he ever allowed one?

NO!

Shit, he had been struggling ever since he was a little kid. Jaleena constantly said their mother treated them fairly, but that was a damn lie. His sister always got the best of everything while he was left alone with other family members to find his own way.

So, he started stealing from other people to get what he wanted out of life. It wasn't like the people he robbed didn't have enough money to replace what he took. Now he might have gotten in over his head with all of his wheeling and dealing.

He had borrowed some money from a couple of hardcore loan sharks and he had to find a way to repay them, or his life was over. Why wouldn't Jaleena give him more money? She had it and should give it to him. She was his sister, and that meant giving him what he needed.

Trent was reaching for his beer when his cell phone rang on the bar in front of him. He answered it without checking the caller ID.

"Hello," he said.

"Trent, do you have the money you owe me?" the gruff voice snapped. "Your time is almost up to pay me. You do know how I'll get payment if you don't have the money."

His body unconsciously shivered at the threat, but he kept the fear out of his voice. "Man, I told you that I don't have any money. You have to give me more time. My sister isn't giving me anything. I have to talk to her again."

"I'm not concerned about how you get my money, as long as you get it." The phone clicked dead on the other end.

He snapped his phone closed and tossed it back on the bar. Shit, what was he going to do now? He took another sip of his drink and thought about his sister. Maybe Jaleena was right. He never wanted to do anything good with his life, not even when he was a kid. He was constantly searching for the quick fix and look where it had gotten him. Nothing to even brag about or show for it, he was truly a lost cause.

Jaleena had spent her money right. She had her own business. Sure, he still thought *Talk of the Town* was a junk yard and she was trying to relive her childhood with all of that crap, but at least it was hers.

She had been there for him so much, and what did he do in return? He had tried to hurt her. He should have gone back and apologized. She might even have forgiven him and gave him some extra money, but that wasn't going to happen now. That stupid plumber had to bring his ass all up in their business, and now his sister wasn't even taking his phone calls. He wouldn't be able to get extra money to repay his debts. Now he had to get out of town quick and his sister's new boyfriend was to blame.

"I'm not going to let him get away with messing with

my sister's mind. I'm going to make him pay and it's going to be good, too." Trent tossed back the rest of his drink, placed the glass back down on the counter and left the bar.

Chapter Twenty-One

It was well past five o'clock and closing time, yet Jaleena wasn't about to close with all the customers she still had inside her shop. She couldn't believe how well those flyers had increased her business. She had only put them out yesterday, but when she got to work this morning people were standing outside waiting for her to open up.

Even a few members from her local church had come by and volunteered to help her with anything she might need. She was just taken aback by how well everyone was getting along today.

It was rather crowded, but no one was acting up or causing trouble. It was very refreshing to have this kind of peace. Her brother not being here to start something could have been the reason, too. It seemed like wherever he went, trouble followed because he didn't know how to tell certain people no.

From the corner of her eye, Jaleena noticed a young teenage girl having a problem finding a price on a digital camera. She left the front of the shop and headed for the electronics section. It was her hottest section of the store today and she didn't want to miss out on a sale. She was halfway there when she heard someone scream.

"Where in the hell is that thief who stole my divan and is selling it in this crappy ass junkyard! I want to speak to her now!" the outraged female voice yelled.

Spinning around, Jaleena spotted a tall, elegant woman standing by the door of her store waving one of her flyers in the air. "I want an answer! Where is this person?"

Everyone in the place turned and looked in her direction. She didn't know what to do. Why was this woman saying she stole her stuff? She hadn't taken anything. She had to take care of this before it got out of hand. She didn't need this woman scaring off all of her customers.

"Ma'am, I'm Jaleena Falcon. I own *Talk of the Town*. How may I help you?" She moved towards the woman as she forgot about the customer who needed her assistance.

The woman frowned at her as she stopped circling the flyer over her head. "Excuse me...are you talking to me?"

"Yes, I heard you accuse the owner of being a thief. I'm not a thief. I didn't take anything. I hope we can get to the bottom of this problem. If you need a deal on something in here we can talk," Jaleena said, pausing in front of the woman.

"Do you know who I am? I'm Caitlin Alexander. I don't buy cheap, used, or secondhand ever. I can buy it right off the showroom floor. I wouldn't ever want someone like you to give me a bargain on anything you have in this dump, but I'll be more than happy to tell everyone here that you're a thief."

Jaleena took a deep breath and tried to relax her pounding heart and racing nerves. She wanted to go off on this

Caitlin woman, but that wouldn't help her. She had to find out why this woman acted this away, and being calm was the only way to do it.

"What have I supposedly taken from you?"

"Do you see that black divan over there in the corner with the sticker for eight hundred dollars?"

"Yes," Jaleena answered. "I know it quite well."

"It's worth three times that easily. I was told my movers had lost it, but I see now that was a lie. They gave it to you to sell in this place. I want someone to call the police so I can have you arrested for fencing stolen property," Caitlin snapped.

The divan she found abandoned at the side of the road belonged to this crazy woman in front of her. Jaleena couldn't believe her luck. Jaleena had assumed somebody threw out the divan, and never considered the movers might have lost it for a customer. Now, she had to deal with somebody claiming to have bought it, causing all kinds of problems and threatening to toss her ass in jail.

"Mrs. Alexander, I'm sure we can work something out if you have a receipt for the divan, or the phone number for the movers. There is no need to get the police involved."

"No!" Caitlin yelled at her. "I want you taken to jail and I'm not going to settle for anything less than that."

Fear settled in Jaleena as she got a good look at the woman's eyes. There was a lot of hate in there, and she knew she couldn't reason with her at all. She was only selling a divan she found tossed on the side of the road.

She was so lost in thought that she didn't notice Ridge coming up behind the woman until he spoke.

"Caitlin, I don't think you have to get the police involved. I'm positive that Jaleena didn't know the divan was yours," Ridge said. "Why don't you calm down and listen to her instead of causing a problem? Do you see how everyone is looking at you? Does a woman of your status really want to be the main gossip of the week?"

She watched as Caitlin twirled around so fast that she almost fell over. "Ridge, what are you doing here?"

☙❧

Ridge hated that Jaleena met his ex-girlfriend before he got a chance to tell her about Caitlin, but they had been having such a wonderful time learning about each other that he honestly hadn't wanted to ruin it by bringing her up. Yet, the lapse in his bad judgment came back to haunt him. Caitlin was here, about to show his girlfriend the side of her he hated, and there was nothing he could do about it.

"I'm here supporting my girlfriend. She needed me here and I'm here," he replied.

Caitlin eyed him up and down a couple of times, then glanced back at Jaleena. "Is she the reason you're wearing a suit, too? I could never get you to wear one for me unless I pleaded with you for a week. What's so damn special about her?"

"I don't have to answer you, but I will. We are going out to dinner after Jaleena closes up her shop." Ridge noticed how the customers were slowly easing out the door in case something blew up. He guessed they didn't want to be witnesses to a crime. Caitlin wasn't a violent person, but she didn't know how to keep her mouth shut. She thought her money and status made it all right for her to belittle people anytime she got the chance.

"You never went out of your way for me like this," she complained. "I only wonder why you would do it for her." Caitlin pointed a manicured finger over her shoulder at a shocked Jaleena. "Was she the one you were with that time I called you?"

Ridge saw how Jaleena listened to every word said between them. He had to take care of this or Caitlin wasn't going to give up. "Let me pay you for the divan. I know Jaleena wasn't trying to take anything from you. We just want to be left alone so we can move on with our relationship."

"You think you're in love with this woman?" Caitlin demanded. "You can't have known her long enough to have developed those types of feelings. Besides, I know you can't have that much in common with her."

"It doesn't take long to fall in love with someone. Sometimes you just know you found *the one*." He smiled at Jaleena and was thrilled when she smiled back at him.

"I can't believe you want to embarrass me like this. You are really offering me money for the loveseat. What if I don't want money from you? What if I'd rather have you instead? She can keep the damn piece of furniture!"

"Caitlin, it isn't going to make any difference. I'm not in love with you. I've never been in love with you. I told you that from the beginning. We have been over for weeks now."

"No, you're just trying to make me jealous. I'll forgive you. Let's leave and I'll treat you to dinner."

Ridge hated how desperate Caitlin was acting. Her attitude wasn't going to change his mind; he wasn't going to leave with her. "Stop this and leave with some dignity."

Caitlin's eyes turned cold as she glared at him. Ridge believed that his words were finally getting through to his ex-girlfriend. He only hoped that it would last this time and she wouldn't try to worm herself back into his life.

"Fine," she hissed. "I was trying to make you into

something better than you were, but I see that you enjoy being on the bottom. Stay here with the other trash and see how far that gets you." Caitlin brushed past him and stormed out the front door.

"How much do you want for the divan?" Ridge yelled after her.

"Keep it. It's truly a piece of junk now after it's been in this godawful place," she hollered back. "Why don't you stay here with her? I don't want you touching me after you have been with something like her. I would feel dirty."

Ridge watched through the glass window of Jaleena's shop as Caitlin got into her car and drove off. She was so pissed at him that there was no telling what kind of rumors she would spread about him throughout the community, but he didn't care. He couldn't stand by and allow her to speak to his woman like that. She knew nothing about Jaleena, and for her to act like she did was very insulting.

"Wow, your ex-girlfriend is something else. I don't think I have ever seen a woman that mad before," Jaleena said.

"I'm sorry that happened to you. Caitlin had no business storming in here like that and scaring off all of your customers. She probably cost you a lot of money today, and future sales."

"Oh, I'm not worrying about it. I'm pretty sure that the gossip from today will have people coming in to get a look at the woman with the Scarlet A across her forehead. This is a small town and something like this will be talked about for months. I might actually make more money because of it."

"I guess I arrived in the nick of time, before it got any worse," he said. "Caitlin can be a handful...no honestly, she can be a real bitch most of the time, but I want you to know that I had broken up with her *way* before I asked you out on a date."

"I never thought you were cheating on me. You don't come across like a man who would date two women at the same time."

Moving closer to Jaleena, Ridge wrapped her up in his arms. "Baby, you are the only woman I want in my life. Do you know how beautiful you truly are? You always have a smile on your face. It makes me so happy just being around you."

"Can I take you home with me?" Jaleena asked, then gave him a quick kiss. "You are so good for my ego. I haven't had a man give me compliments the way you do. I think I could get used to having you around for a very long time."

"Good, I wasn't planning on going anywhere," Ridge said, stepping back from her.

"Thank you."

"You don't have to thank me for speaking the truth."

"No, I was thanking you for taking care of your ex-girlfriend. I thought she really was going to call the police and have me tossed in jail. She acted like the both of you were too good to be in my 'junkyard.' I'm not quite sure if I quoted her correctly or not, but it was close enough."

"I'm sorry Caitlin hurt your feelings. You didn't deserve to be talked to like that." He reached for her again, but she swatted his hands away.

"I'm not that sensitive. I promise you I'm not going to cry. Caitlin has a right to her opinion. After dealing with my crazy brother all of these years, I can handle just about anyone or anything. I'm very strong. Let me get this place closed up and we can go out to dinner, my treat."

Ridge watched while Jaleena moved around *Talk of the Town* with confidence and closed everything up. He loved how proud she was of this place. Each day made him so happy that he found her and made her a part of his life. She was the perfect woman for him. He couldn't wait until he introduced her to Billy. He wasn't sure how well his uncle would react to her, because he was raised back in the day when the two races didn't mix.

But, he was sure that Billy would love Jaleena just as much as he did. He couldn't wait until he got the two of them into the same room, but for now he had an idea of how he wanted to spend the night with his woman.

Reaching inside his pants pocket, he pulled out his cell phone and turned it off before tossing it down on the counter. He didn't want any interruptions tonight from anyone.

Strolling across the room, he wrapped his arms around Jaleena's waist and planted a kiss on the back of her neck. "I was thinking about something."

"What is it?" Jaleena asked, leaning back against his chest.

"I have wanted a new couch for a while; however, I never saw one I wanted to get until now. How about I take this one off of your hands? It would go perfectly downstairs in my basement. I can lay on it and watch all the sports that I want."

"You really want your ex-girlfriend's furniture in your house, if it's hers?"

"It was never in Caitlin's house, but I have a suggestion how to make it ours," he whispered by her ear.

"What is your suggestion, Mr. Taylor?"

"Let's make it ours."

"How do you suggest we do that?"

Spinning her around, Ridge picked Jaleena up in his arms and carried her over to the black divan in the center of the room. He tossed her down on it and covered her body quickly with his. "I think we should make love on it."

"I like the way your mind works," Jaleena said as she pulled his face towards hers.

"So do I, sweetheart," Ridge answered before kissing his girlfriend.

∽≈

Not once while they were getting lost in each other did Ridge or Jaleena feel a pair of eyes watching them from through the crack in blinds in the front of the store.

"How dare they be in there like that without a care in the world when my life is falling apart? I'm going to make both of them pay for doing this to me. I'll teach them a lesson that they will never forget."

The person peeked at them one last time before easing away from the window and blending into the darkness.

Chapter Twenty-Two

"Good morning, sweetheart," a voice whispered before a warm kiss touched her temple.

Opening her eyes, Jaleena gazed at Ridge sitting on the bed next to her, fully dressed. "Hi yourself," she replied softly. "How long have you been sitting there staring at me? I know I must look like something the cat dragged in." She slid up in bed and rested against the headboard, and brushed down her hair with her hands.

"I have only been here for a few minutes. I love watching you sleep. You look so peaceful. I really didn't want to wake you up, but I wanted to treat you to breakfast. How does that sound?" Ridge kissed her on the lips before she could move out of the way.

"God, why did you do that? I don't want to kill you with my morning breath."

"Jaleena, I love your morning breath and all, don't you know that by now?"

Her heart skipped a beat, hearing Ridge's words, which she had been thinking about for a while now. "I love you, too."

"I kind of thought you did, but it's good to hear." He leaned in to kiss her again, but his cell phone went off before their lips met.

"Keep that thought," Ridge laughed as he held up a finger. He pulled his phone out and glanced at it. She noticed a frown cover his handsome face.

"What is it?"

"It's the hospital," he replied. "I don't know why they could be calling me."

"Answer it." Jaleena waved at the phone in Ridge's hand.

"Okay," he said. "Hello?"

Jaleena tried to hear what was going on, but she couldn't make out what the other person was saying to Ridge. She just saw the color drain from his face, and in her heart she knew that something was horribly wrong.

"I'll be right there," Ridge uttered, then hung up the phone.

"Baby, what's wrong?" she asked, moving closer to Ridge and placing her hand on his leg. "Tell me."

"My Uncle Billy got shot last night. He's in serious condition. They tried calling me when it happened, but they couldn't get me. There's no message from Hank. I bet he doesn't know yet."

"Oh, my God." Jaleena jumped out of bed and started yanking clothes out of her closet. "Let me get dressed. I'll drive you to the hospital."

"You don't have to do that."

"Yes, I do. You aren't in any condition to drive." Jaleena tossed on some clothes and grabbed her purse. "Come on, let's go." She rushed out of her bedroom door and down the hall for the front door with Ridge right behind her.

∽∾

The drive to the hospital seemed like it took hours. Jaleena sent up a silent prayer of thanks that she found a parking spot near the front door. She turned in her seat and noticed the lost and haunted look in Ridge's usually bright eyes.

"Honey, your Uncle Billy is going to be just fine," she promised, placing her hand on top of Ridge's cold one. "Go inside and I'll find you. You need a few minutes alone with Billy."

"Are you sure?" Ridge asked as he finally looked at her. "I wanted the two of you to meet, but not like this."

"Yes, you go ahead. I'll be in right behind you." Jaleena gave Ridge a gentle shove. He couldn't go into shock now. Billy needed him too much.

Ridge kissed her on the mouth, then rushed out of the car towards the front entrance. Jaleena watched him until he was out of sight. Dropping her head down on the steering wheel, she remembered how scared she was when she got the phone call about her mother.

It had been the worst night of her life. She prayed that Ridge didn't have to go through the same thing. Sure, Billy wasn't his parent, but he was closest thing to it and her boyfriend loved his uncle so much.

Doubts entered her mind. Was she the reason Ridge wasn't able to get here last night, because he was spending it with her at *Talk of the Town* and back at her place? Ridge turned off his phone for her and that was something he said he *never* did, until yesterday.

"I can't stay out here thinking about what ifs. Ridge needs me in there with him and that is where I'm going."

Jaleena composed herself a little more before she left the car and went in search of Ridge.

Inside the hospital, she looked around the waiting room, then finally asked a nurse who pointed her in the right direction of Billy's room. Jaleena spotted Ridge looking at Billy through a window in the door. She could tell that he didn't know she was there yet. She eased up next to him and put her hand inside of his. Ridge turned his head and looked at her. She saw the tears in his eyes.

"How is he doing?"

☙❧

Looking down into Jaleena's upturned face, Ridge knew he had found the woman he was meant to spend the rest of his life with. She was here with him showing true concern for Billy. It felt wonderful to have the love of a good woman. Now that he had Jaleena, it was time he took care of Billy. He knew that Billy was getting too old to do this job, but he hadn't spoken up. Yet, he was going to do it now. He didn't care if Billy threw a fit at him. He wasn't going to let him do any more late night jobs.

"The nurse said he's no longer in serious condition and that he's been opening his eyes off and on during the night. I'm still upset I wasn't here when they brought him in. I hate to think of him being scared and all alone. I promise that I won't do anything else to hurt or upset him. I'm going to give Billy anything he wants from now on."

"I believe Billy knows how much you care about him," Jaleena said, squeezing Ridge's hand.

"If he doesn't, he will now," Ridge swore, looking away from the window down at Jaleena.

"Ridge, look," she said, pointing at Billy. "I think he's

opening his eyes."

He looked away from Jaleena and back over at Billy. She was right, Billy was opening his eyes. "I should go in there and see him. I want you to come meet him." He moved towards the door, tugging Jaleena behind him.

"No, I think you need to talk to him alone. Find out what happened. I can go back to the waiting room. There will be plenty of time for us to get to know each other." She let go of his hand and stepped back. "Go and be with your family."

"Are you sure?"

"Positive. It's not like I'm going anywhere."

Ridge ran his hand down the side of Jaleena's face and gave her a small smile before he stepped away and rushed inside Billy's hospital room.

CHAPTER TWENTY-THREE

He blinked back tears as he sat down in the chair next to Billy's bed and took his wrinkled hand. He grinned as Billy looked at him. "Old man, you almost gave me a heart attack at my young age. Do you know how bad I felt when the hospital called and told me you had gotten shot? What in the hell happened?"

"What are you crying for, boy?" Billy complained, taking his hand back. "I'm a tough old bird. It's going to take more than a young punk trying to rob us to take me out. I almost had him until he pulled out the gun and shot me."

"Do you know who it was? Did you get a look at his face?" Ridge wasn't going to stop until this person was behind bars.

"Nope, the coward was wearing a mask. I wish had seen his face," his uncle answered. "Did the doctors tell you that if the bullet had been anymore to the left I might not be able to walk?"

Ridge hadn't heard this news yet. He felt his stomach drop to the bottom of his shoes. "Are you going to get movement back in your legs?"

"I tried to move this early this morning when I first woke up, but I couldn't do it. It might be from the swelling in my spine. The doctor told me I might have to be in a wheelchair for a while because he doesn't want me moving too soon and injuring myself more. I'm not getting in any damn chair. I'm not that bad off."

"You will do as the doctor tells you, or I'll glue your ass to the seat if I have to! Do you understand me, Billy?" he warned.

"Ridge, I should never have said anything," Billy groaned, glaring at him. "I'm not an invalid."

"I didn't say you were, but you mean the world to me. I love you and would do anything for you. I tried calling Hank, but kept getting voice mail," Ridge said. "I told him to call the hospital."

"Thanks for calling Hank. But, I hope you know that you mean a lot to me, too, son," his uncle said.

"Enough about me, are you going to tell me why they couldn't get hold of you last night? Were you with Caitlin? I know how controlling she can be when it comes to your time. Did she have you turn off your phone?"

"No…Caitlin and I broke up a while ago," Ridge answered. "We are over for good. I finally saw her for the real person she was. It was hard for her to let me go, but she finally did."

"I tried telling you about her, and you acted like you weren't hearing me. At one time, you told me I should keep my mouth shut."

"I know. I apologized, and enough about Caitlin. I want to tell you about the new woman I'm with. She's the one I've been waiting for. I can't wait until you get to meet her.

You will love her as much as I do."

"Oh, you're dating another cute little blonde," Billy said, giving him a devilish look. "I know how much you love them. I can't wait until I see her. Back in the day, I was a blonde man myself. There is just something about them that can get to a man, don't you agree?"

"What if she isn't blonde?" Ridge asked. He was slowly getting a sick feeling in the pit of his stomach.

"A brunette or redhead is fine, too."

"Uncle Billy, I need to tell you something about my girlfriend Jaleena."

Billy frowned at him and then turned up his nose like he had a bad taste in his mouth. "Jaleena, what kind of name is that?" he asked.

"I think it's a beautiful name and it fits her perfectly."

"You aren't telling me something. What is it?"

Ridge closed his eyes and prayed that Billy wouldn't react the way he was thinking he would. He opened his eyes and looked directly at his uncle. "Billy, Jaleena is black. I'm in love with her and I'm going to ask her to marry me."

"Hell, no," Billy yelled at him. "I won't let you do it. You can't let yourself get hooked up with one of them. I'd rather you be with Caitlin than a black woman."

"Billy, I love her and I'm going to marry Jaleena," Ridge tossed back.

"I'm not going to stand for this. So, you are going to have to choose either your new girlfriend or me."

How could his uncle ask him to do something like this? There was no way he could choose between the two people he loved the most in this world. It just wasn't possible. He didn't know what to do.

How could Billy put him in a situation like this? He

loved both his uncle and Jaleena equally and with everything in him. Why should he have one person in his life and not the other one? His uncle had been in his life for so long that he couldn't remember a time that he wasn't. On the other hand, Jaleena made his heart beat faster and his mood lightened anytime he was in her presence. He loved just being around her.

Her love had given him a new lease on life. She was the polar opposite of every woman he had been with since he was sixteen years old.

Could he really go on with the rest of his life without her?

He looked at Billy lying in the hospital bed, looking fragile and watching him, and he knew what he had to do. As much as he hated it, this had to be done and with the least amount of pain as possible. He made a promise and he was going to keep it, no matter how much it killed him to do so.

Ridge slowly got up from the chair like he had the weight of the world on his shoulders. "I'll be right back."

"Where are you going?" Billy asked. "You are about to do something that will affect both of us are you, boy? Listen to me…I know what you want, but I think…."

"Don't worry about it. I'll be right back." Ridge walked out the door in search of Jaleena.

Flipping through a book, Jaleena barely saw what was in front of her because she was waiting for Ridge to come back from seeing Billy. She was about to go and check in on him when she felt someone staring at her. Glancing up, she spotted Ridge standing in front of her. She tossed the book down on the chair next to her.

The tired look on his face broke her heart. He looked so worn out, and they had only been at the hospital for an hour. He had been there for her through the Caitlin incident, now it was time for her to be there for him.

"How is your Uncle Billy doing? Is he going to be okay? Does he have any clue who shot him?"

Ridge's gaze ran up and down her body a few times before he finally answered her. "He's going to be okay, but he is going to need some extra care for the next couple of months." It will probably fall to me to take care of it, since I don't know if Hank will be able to move back and do it."

"I understand and I'm here for you. I don't mind helping out where I can," she said. "Are you ready for me to meet him?"

"He's not up to any visitors right now," he answered, then glanced away from her.

"What are you keeping from me? Is he worse than you first thought? God, Ridge you can tell me. Don't you know how much I want to help you anyway that I can?"

"No, he isn't worse. He was actually awake and he talked to me," Ridge answered her.

Jaleena slowly got the feeling that Ridge wasn't telling her everything. She wanted to know what was going on with him. He wasn't acting like himself at all. "If your uncle isn't up for visitors I can understand, and I can wait to meet him later when he's feeling better."

"I was telling Billy about you," Ridge said.

"Did he say something to you about not wanting to meet me?" Jaleena asked. "You know that you can tell me anything and we can work through it."

Ridge ran his fingers through his hair and blew out a

deep breath. "He was very excited about meeting my new girlfriend until I told him that you were..."

"A black woman?" Jaleena filled in the word for Ridge as she stood up. "He doesn't want me around you or him now? Is that it?"

"Yes, he told me that I had to choose between the two of you."

"You picked him over me, didn't you?" Jaleena gasped, softly as sudden hurt filled her heart. She didn't need to be told the truth. She could tell from his body language what his decision was without hearing the words.

"Jaleena, don't take this personally. Don't let my uncle get to you like this. Billy has been through a lot in twenty-four hours. Please give him time. He'll come around and love you as much as I do." Ridge reached for her, but she moved away from him.

"No, don't touch me," she said, shaking her head.

"I promise when he's back to his old self I'll make him listen about us. Please don't get upset about this. I wouldn't be able to stand it if I hurt you. I just need to be with him right now. Uncle Billy raised me while Hank was away in the military. I was supposed to be at work last night instead of him. He got shot because I wasn't there, and if he needs me to hold his hand for a little while then I'll do it."

"Ridge, when you came out here to tell me these things it was over between us. You already put the nail in your coffin. Time isn't going to change Billy's mind. People like him never see their views as wrong."

"Jaleena, don't be like this," Ridge said, his eyes pleading with her. "Why can't you see this my way just this once and not make it more than it is? I didn't hold your brother against you, did I? Why can't you be the same way with me?"

"I'll pray for him, but after he is well please don't come looking for me. I'll make sure to lose your phone number and I want you to do the same with mine."

Jaleena walked away from Ridge with her head held high and not once did she look back at him. Oh, she wanted to with everything she had in her, especially when he yelled her name, but her willpower was stronger. She kept going until she got inside her car, and that was when she finally let the tears fall.

Ridge stood rooted to the spot where he dumped Jaleena long after she had disappeared from sight. He still couldn't believe he had done something so stupid. What was wrong with him? He shouldn't let Billy have the kind of power over him, but with Hank not here his uncle was the only family he had left in town, and right now Billy needed him.

"I'm not going to lose her. I will get her back," he promised himself

Jaleena was the love of his life and a connection like theirs couldn't be killed with a few misunderstood words. Once she calmed down, she would see that what he did wasn't all that bad. He only told Billy that he would break things off with Jaleena so he could help him recover from being shot. He didn't think it would take that long until his uncle was up and back on his feet. Ridge knew he would be back on Jaleena's doorstep, begging her to understand why he did what he did. She had to take him back because Jaleena loved him too much not to do it.

Spinning on his heel, Ridge headed back towards his Uncle Billy's room when his cell phone rang. He pulled it out of the front pocket of his jeans and answered it.

"Hello?"

"Ridge, I heard about your Uncle Billy. Is he okay?" Caitlin asked. "Do you need me to come to the hospital? I can sit there with you while he's asleep or I can bring you something to eat, sweetheart."

He held the phone away from his ear and glared at it before bringing it back to his face. "Tell me the truth. How did you really find out about my uncle's hospital stay? He called you, didn't he?" he demanded in a low voice as he headed towards an exit sign when a nurse gave him a look.

Outside, Ridge glanced around, hoping to spot Jaleena's car, but it was nowhere in sight. The one woman he wanted to talk to was gone and now he was on the phone with the one he could care less about.

Why was the world trying to screw him over?

"Yes, your uncle called me," she admitted. "He was concerned about what was going on between you and that Jaleena woman. See, I'm not the only one who sees that you shouldn't be with her. God, what has gotten into you? I never saw you as the type to go to the other side.

"Honey, I forgive you for cheating on me. I understand how men can get a little nervous in a committed relationship and might need to test other waters. Just apologize to me and everything will be great between us. The Mayor's Ball is in a couple of weeks, so why don't we get you fitted for that tuxedo and forget all of this happened?"

Anger took over his body, making his blood race through his veins. Ridge couldn't believe that Caitlin had the nerve to tell him that she forgave him. What in the fuck was wrong with her? They weren't a couple anymore and hadn't been for weeks. Did she actually have something mentally wrong with her, and that was the reason she didn't understand the words coming out of his mouth?

Hell, she even tossed him to Jaleena after she found him at *Talk of the Town*. How could she have forgotten the fit she had thrown in front of everyone, causing Jaleena to lose customers? He had to truly deal with this craziness for once and all, or Caitlin would keep turning up in his life like a bad penny, and that wasn't something that he needed or wanted.

"Caitlin, I want you to listen to me very closely. I have lost count of the times I have told you this. So, understand this is the very last time we are going to have this conversation. We aren't in a relationship. We never were—all we did was have sex when both of us needed to let off some steam after a hard day. I'm not going to a party at the mayor's with you. Whatever my Uncle Billy told you wasn't from me. I don't want you back in my life. If you see me out with Jaleena, walk the other way and don't cause us any problems.

"I'm in love with Jaleena and I believe I have ruined things with her by listening to my uncle. I made a promise to him and I will keep it. However, as soon as he gets better and is back on his feet, I'm going after the woman I'm madly in love with. Hopefully, she won't be too angry with me and she'll take me back.

"You don't have a place in my life and never will. So, will you finally get it through your head to leave what you thought we had in the past? Caitlin, you're an attractive woman. Why don't you take all of the energy you're using towards me and get out there? I know you can get any man you want, but he isn't me."

"You're really in love with her, aren't you?" she asked in a low voice. "You weren't trying to make me jealous?"

"No, I wasn't trying to make you jealous," Ridge answered. "I want Jaleena and no one else."

"Don't worry. I won't bother you anymore. Why would I when another woman has your heart. Goodbye, Ridge." Caitlin ended the phone call before he could say another word.

Ridge hung up on his end and then slid the phone back into his pocket. He felt like a huge weight had been lifted off his shoulders. Now, all he had to do was get his Uncle Billy well and he would be back at Jaleena's door, begging for forgiveness. Hopefully, she would take pity on him and take him back pretty quickly.

Turning on his heel, he started back towards the hospital entrance, already thinking about what he would pack up to stay with his uncle until he was back on his feet. He prayed that his recovery wouldn't take as long as the doctors had told him. He didn't want too much time to pass before he could fix things with Jaleena.

CHAPTER TWENTY-FOUR

One year later...
New Year's Eve.

Walking around *Talk of the Town*, Jaleena worked on pricing all of the items that were going to be in her New Year's Day sale tomorrow. She wanted to get everything done before he woke up. It had taken a better part of the night before he finally got to sleep at home. Since she didn't have anyone to watch him, she decided to start bringing him to work with her.

She was almost done when the sound of a baby crying echoed through her store. Jaleena put down the roll of price stickers and made her way over to the bassinet at the side of her desk. She picked up her son and patted him on the back.

"Shhh....Aden, it's going to be okay," she whispered softly in his ear.

Her baby boy calmed down instantly at the sound of her voice and soothing touch. "Let me go and fix your bottle. I know you're hungry. Mama's sorry that she took so long with those price tags.

"I'll be here sooner next time. I'm just trying to get ready for my huge sale. Don't you want us to make a lot of money?" Jaleena asked her infant son like he was actually going to answer her back.

"CeCe, didn't you hear Aden crying?" she asked her new assistant as she came from the back room carrying two lamps.

"I'm sorry, Ms. Falcon," CeCe apologized. "I was in the back getting these lamps out for the sale this weekend. I didn't hear him. You know I wouldn't let him cry. He was asleep when I last checked on him."

"That's okay," Jaleena said. "I think he wanted to spend some time with his mama. You know how my little man can be sometimes. After you put those lamps down, can you finish working on that roll of stickers? I need prices placed on all of the items over there on the table in front of the bay window. I want to draw as many customers in that I can. I left them on my desk out front."

"I'll get right on it," CeCe said as she walked past her.

"Thank you." Jaleena smiled at CeCe before she headed for the back to fix Aden a bottle.

She loved her son so much. He looked so much like his father with his gray eyes and dark brown hair. She was completely shocked to find out she was pregnant weeks after Ridge dumped her at the hospital. She guessed that time they had made love on the black divan was when it happened, because that was the only time Ridge hadn't used a condom. Her mother was right—it only took one time for it to happen.

More than once she had reached for the phone to call and tell him about the baby, but in the end she decided it would be in Aden's best interest not to be around Ridge because of his uncle.

Besides her being pregnant with Ridge's baby and dealing with his rejection, she got a visit from the local police. Somehow they had gotten hold of a surveillance video that proved her brother Trent was the person who had robbed Billy and shot him. After finding out there was a warrant for his arrest, her brother had gone on the run and they thought she knew where he was hiding out.

It had taken weeks of going back and forth to the police station before the cops finally believed she was clueless as to Trent's whereabouts, and they left her alone.

Honestly, she didn't care if she ever saw Trent again. He had brought too much pain into her life, and it was way past time that she cut the cord to their relationship. She was only his sister and not his mother. She had her own child to take care of now, and that was her main responsibility.

Yet, a part of her hated not having Ridge in her life—she missed him way more than she was willing to admit. Honestly, she was still in love with him, and it hurt that he could toss her away so easily. Since she didn't want to stay in the house and let her mind be filled with thoughts of him, she had gotten more involved with volunteering.

Being around different people in need at some of the local churches and shelters helped her see her life was so much better than she thought. It also helped to get her mind off of Aden's daddy some, but not a lot. He was still lurking there late at night when she was alone in her bed and his son was asleep in his crib.

Pushing Ridge to the back of her mind for the moment, Jaleena moved around the small makeshift kitchen. She worked on getting Aden's bottle ready while he made baby sounds against her shoulder.

Her son was truly the most perfect gift that she could have ever wished for. Her mother would be so in love with her grandson, and would have spoiled him to death with way too many gifts, like most proud grandparents do.

Once Aden's bottle was fixed, she sat down at her the table in the corner in the kitchen and fed him. He took the bottle instantly, watching her as he snuggled closer to her. She smiled down at her son, loving the change he had brought into her life. He was her world now and nothing else mattered but making sure he was well taken care of.

Ridge should know about him. Tell him, her mind thought.

Jaleena pushed the sudden thought out of her head. She wasn't ready to see Ridge yet. Actually, she was scared that he might want to take Aden away from her, especially after the death of his Uncle Billy. After Aden was born she had read in the newspaper that he had passed away, and she eventually found out he had a gotten a bad infection because of the bullet they couldn't get out of his body, and died from a massive heart attack at home.

She thought about going to see Ridge, but after Billy's death but she couldn't bring himself to do it. She couldn't put any more on her plate and she wasn't ready to look Ridge in the eye, not after he had tossed their love away to please his uncle. She hadn't meant enough to him to fight for their love. So, why would he care anything about the child they had created after a night of passion?

For months, Jaleena allowed herself to think about Ridge even when she didn't want to do it, but it was hard to forget someone when all they had going between them was a wicked attraction. The instant they saw each other, it was like fireworks going off around them and she couldn't have fought it. No matter how much she had wanted to ignore him, he had a way about him that would be hard for any woman to ignore.

Glancing down at Aden, she noticed he had fallen back to sleep. She eased the bottle out of his mouth and placed it down on the table. She laid him over her shoulder and gently rubbed his back. He loved getting his back rubbed after getting a bottle; it didn't matter if he was awake or asleep. It was something that lured him deeper into sleep.

"Is he asleep?"

Jaleena glanced to her left and found CeCe standing there with today's mail in her hands.

"Yes, he's out like a light. Can you take him and place him inside his bassinet? I can take a longer break and read the mail while I'm back here. You know if you need any help just ring the phone and I'll come right up front."

"Sure, I can take the little guy." CeCe took Aden from her and handed her the mail. She ran her hand over Aden's soft hair before her assistant walked away with him.

Relaxing back in the seat, Jaleena flipped through the mail, tossing the junk down on the table until her eyes spotted something with a prison postmark across the top. Her hands shook as she looked at the letter for a few seconds. She hadn't heard from her brother since he was arrested for shooting Ridge's uncle. Originally charged with robbery and assault with a deadly weapon, Trent was then charged with murder after Billy died. She refused to attend any hearings or follow the case, so she didn't even know when he'd go to trial. All she knew was that he'd been refused bail.

She didn't even know what he could be writing her about. Despite the fact he had done so much wrong in his life, she still loved him and a part of her was sad Trent couldn't make more out of his life.

Blowing out a deep breath, Jaleena prepared herself for what she was about to read. She tore open the thick letter. Pulling out the sheets of paper, she read.

Hey little sister,

I really thought long and hard before I picked up this pen and paper. I know you weren't expecting to hear from me, and I can't blame you if you don't read this letter any further. If you decide to tear it up and throw it away I understand completely.

How can I apologize to you for everything I have done to you and against you? I know I haven't been a good big brother, and I am sorry.

Ever since I was a little kid I just couldn't seem to do anything right, and I know a lot of it came from not wanting to listen and follow the rules mama set for us.

I always blamed you or mama for my continuing problems with the law when I knew it was my fault. I wasn't living the life mama wanted me to have, but I just didn't care because I wanted my friends to like me. Fitting in with them was more important than listening to anything she was trying to tell me.

Jaleena, I want to tell you how truly sorry I am for dragging you into my problems while you were pregnant with little Aden. Yeah, I know you had a baby. A few of my so co-called friends are in here with me. They told me about my nephew and how the cops thought you knew where I was hiding out. I can't believe they would ever think you would protect me after I shot Ridge's uncle. They don't know how honest you are.

I know you won't believe this, but I do love you. I had a horrible way of showing it. I guess it's because I was so jealous of you. You constantly knew what you wanted since you were a little girl, while I was searching for something with the wrong types of people. Mama knew you were special from the day you were born and you lived up to all of her praises.

Jaleena brushed away tears as she read her brother's confession, but she didn't stop reading his letter. She couldn't believe Trent was being this open and honest with her after giving her so many problems after their mother died.

I shot the old man for two reasons: I hated Ridge from the first day that I met him. I was pissed as hell that he was trying to tell me what to do and how to treat my own sister. He didn't have the right to get involved in our family business. He was a fucking stranger and should have kept his damn mouth shut and stayed in his place. After our run-in, all I could think about was ways to make him pay. I wasn't sure how I was going to do it. I only knew I would get him back.

He never knew I had been following him for a while, and saw him with that old man at his plumbing business. So, a plan began to form in my mind to get back at Ridge. I had to wait for the perfect opportunity and it came sooner than I thought. The last night you had your big sale, I saw you with him on that black couch and I got my opening to get him back for butting his nose in my business.

I made my way over to his plumbing business, broke inside, and robbed them because I needed the money. I owed people and they were threatening to kill me. So, I thought I could get it from that plumber since you weren't about to give me any more. I was on my way out the back door when Billy showed up. I thought I had scared him enough with the gun not to fight me, but he grabbed for it and I shot him.

I was so scared that I just snatched up the money off the floor went around his body and out the door. If you are with Ridge, please tell him how sorry my actions caused his uncle to die.

I'm truly sorry that I dragged you into all of this. I hope one day that you can find it in your heart to forgive me and maybe let me see my nephew.

I guess you probably had a lot of questions running around in your head. I hope that I answered most of them with this letter.
Your brother,
Trent.

Folding up the letter, Jaleena slid it back into the envelope and laid it back on the table in front of us. She couldn't believe what she had just read in her brother's letter. How was she supposed to handle all of this? Why was Trent telling her all of this now?

Why didn't he tell her some of those things before he got sent to prison? She might have understood why he resented her so much when they had been growing up.

Thought after thought raced through her head as she decided whether she should see Ridge. His uncle was the victim of her brother's crime, and maybe knowing some of the reasons why Trent had done it would help him heal.

She had to do this. As much as seeing Ridge again might be painful after a year, so would taking the letter to him. He deserved to know the truth, and if he wasn't at work then she would just leave it there. Jaleena prayed that if she had to see Ridge face to face that she would be able to keep her emotions in check.

They hadn't been together for a year, and he was probably dating someone else. Falling apart in front of him wouldn't do either one of them any good. She wasn't the type to lose control like that, anyway, so it wouldn't happen no matter how good he might look standing in front of her.

Jaleena picked up the letter off the table and stood. She walked towards the front of the building and found CeCe at the desk. Her assistant was working on yesterday's receipts since her business was closed today in order to get ready for the sale tomorrow.

"Do you think you can watch Aden for a while?" she asked, stopping next to her. "I need to go out for a few minutes. I will be back before you have to leave for your other job."

CeCe glanced up from her work and looked at her. "Are you okay, Jaleena? You look a little odd."

"Yes, I'm fine. I just really need to head out and take care of something I got in the mail. Aden has been fed so he should stay asleep until I get back. In case he wakes up and wants another bottle, I have one already made up in the refrigerator. All you have to do is warm it up and give it to him."

Laying the pen down on the desk, CeCe nodded. "Yes, I can handle everything while you're gone. Aden has never been a problem for me before and I doubt that he will be while you aren't here.

"He's a very sweet and calm baby. I love watching him for you. Just do what you need to and we will be here when you get back. Do you mind me asking where you're going?"

"I just need to make some things right with someone so we both will be able to move on," Jaleena answered as she walked towards the exit.

Chapter Twenty-Five

Biting her bottom lip, Jaleena tried to get her nerves under control as she sat in her car, staring at the building to her left. She had lost track of time, so she wasn't positive how long she had been there. She never thought she would be here, especially after the way things ended between the two of them.

Ridge had been out of her world for so long, she didn't even know how things would go between the two of them. What if he just looked at her and kicked her out before one word left her mouth?

She came here for a reason and she wouldn't leave until she did what she came here to do. Looking at the business brought back a pain she wasn't ready to deal with, but she had to do it because of her brother and his actions. Ridge needed to know the truth about everything, and she was the only person who could tell him. All she had to do was make sure that he couldn't tell that she was still in love with him.

Hopefully, no one was in there with him, especially not that bitch Caitlin. For weeks after Ridge had dumped her, she wondered if they were together. Then she found out she was pregnant and the thought of them together left her mind completely.

She really had two things to get out in the open today. Opening up her purse, Jaleena looked at the smaller envelope that held pictures of her baby Aden. She couldn't keep him a secret from Ridge any longer. He needed to know that he was a father of a healthy, adorable baby boy.

Taking a deep breath, she brushed her hair off her face, got out of the vehicle, and made her way towards Ridge's plumbing business. She crossed the street and went inside before she talked herself out of doing it. Walking up to the desk, she hit the bell on the counter and waited for someone to come.

It took a few seconds, but a door behind the desk opened and an attractive man who looked a few years older than Ridge walked out. She heard that Ridge had hired someone to take his uncle's place, and this must be the guy.

She was shocked to see how much he looked like an older version of Ridge. He had to be a family member, but she thought Ridge was an only child. What was going on here?

"Yes, ma'am. Can I help you with something?" the man asked her.

Jaleena continued looking at the guy, wondering if she should ask if was he related to Ridge, but it really wasn't any of her business. He wasn't her boyfriend anymore and nothing in his life was any of her concern.

"Ma'am, is there a reason you're just standing there looking at me? Did you come here looking to have something fixed? My cousin is the main person who does the job, but he isn't here right now. I can take a message if you like. If you leave your name and number I'll give it to Ridge when he gets back from his current job."

"I'm sorry. I was staring at you. I just didn't know Ridge had a cousin that lived in town," Jaleena said. "I knew he had an uncle named Billy."

"Yes, he was my father. My name is Hank. I wasn't aware that you were familiar with my family," he said, staring at her closely. "Do you need a plumber or did you come for another reason?"

After the initial confusion wore off, Jaleena suddenly remembered Ridge talking about his cousin Hank a few times. She secretly wondered, if Hank had been around back then, would she and Ridge have stayed together, but nothing she wished for now could change the past.

"No, I didn't need a plumber," she answered. "I came here to see Ridge."

Hank glanced at his watch then back at her. "My cousin has been gone for a while, so he should he back in a few minutes. You are more than welcome to wait for him. Why don't you have a seat over there?" He pointed to a chair about ten feet away from the door.

Jaleena glanced over at the seat and decided if she waited CeCe might get worried about her. She had to get back to Aden and her business. "Hmmm…I don't think that will be a good idea. I can't stay that long anyway."

She was disappointed Ridge wasn't here, but she guessed it meant he wasn't supposed to find out about Aden. "Like I said, I just came here to see Ridge and give him something, but you can do it for me."

"Miss, I still don't know what you are referring to," Hank said. "Are you sure that you don't have enough time to wait for Ridge? I promise you that he should be back any minute now. The job was across town, but he left over an hour ago."

"Yes, I'm positive that I can't wait any for him to come back." She opened up her purse and pulled Trent's letter out, unaware that another envelope that hit the floor. "Here, will you please give this to him? Tell him to read it and it will explain everything that happened. Look, I really need to leave. I'm so sorry about your father."

Jaleena rushed toward the exit, but turned back to see Hank set aside the letter without looking at it. She wondered if he would notice the prison address and her name, and connect her with the man who shot his father. She got into her car and raced away in case he did.

Chapter Twenty-Six

Ridge was about two buildings away from Taylor's Plumbing when he saw her, but he didn't believe his eyes. He had been dreaming about Jaleena so much that he was now seeing someone who looked like leaving his business and getting into a car.

He couldn't believe how things went downhill so quickly after his uncle was released from the hospital. It seemed like one day Billy was taking physical therapy and getting stronger, and then overnight he had a sudden relapse and was back in the hospital, then three weeks later he was dead. Everything had hit him so hard that he didn't have time to even grieve for his uncle.

The police came looking for him at the hospital to ask about Trent being the shooter and if he could testify about Jaleena's brother's behavior for violence at the trial. After he had testified, he attended some of the hearings, but he never saw her there. He knew he had cut her out of his life, but he hoped to catch a glimpse of her. He was torn between still caring about her and hating Trent for being the reason his uncle was buried six feet under.

Also, Hank wanted Trent to get the longest sentence possible for killing his father. How could he tell his cousin he had been involved with the shooter's sister? While he was trying to figure out what to do about the situation months passed him by and now it was a year later. Why hadn't he just gone to see her?

As much as he wanted to hate Billy for insisting that he break up with Jaleena, he did it, and in the end losing her was all on his shoulders. He couldn't fault anyone else but himself for his stupid mistakes. Now, he was hallucinating her; yet, a part of him secretly wanted to believe that his eyes weren't playing tricks on him, and it had been Jaleena running across the street and getting into that car.

"No, it wasn't her," Ridge said as he watched the car speed off around the corner.

She wouldn't have come to see him, not after all this time. But, what if he was wrong? If it was Jaleena he had to find out why she came by his business and left before he got a chance to talk to her.

Parking his car in front of Taylor's Plumbing, Ridge turned off his truck and didn't waste a moment getting out to find Hank. He had to find out what was going on. The second he got inside the familiar sent of Jaleena's perfume hit his nose.

He never forgot what she smelled like in the year they had been apart. He remembered how the scent of coconut and apricot filled his senses after they made love and snuggled together in his bed. It had been her. She had come to see him and he hadn't been here! Fuck! He should have sent Hank to that stupid job way across town..

"Hank, where are you?" Ridge hollered, closing the

door behind him.

"I'm here," Hank answered, coming out of the back room. "What is all the screaming about? God, I'm not deaf. What's your problem?"

"Who was that woman who just left here? I swear she looked like Jaleena."

"She didn't say. She came by to see you but left when she found out you weren't here," his cousin answered.

"Did she say anything else to you? Why didn't you make her wait for me?" he demanded. "You knew I would be coming back soon. Were you rude to her? I swear if you were, you are going to regret it," he warned.

"Shit, I don't know what you are so upset about. I didn't chase her away, if that's what you're thinking. I was very nice to her, but she just didn't want to wait for you, so calm down."

Ridge looked away from Hank as he tried to get back under control. Hank was right. He wasn't a bigot or anything close to it. He shouldn't have jumped down his cousin's throat.

"Man, I'm sorry. I saw Jaleena as she was leaving. Tell me why she was here."

"I'm not lying to you. I don't why she came to see you, but she did give me this letter to give to you." Hank picked up an envelope off the counter and handed it to him."

Taking the letter, he stared at it for a few seconds. "Why would she give me a letter that her brother sent to her from prison?" Ridge asked. "I don't understand why she needs to think I want to read anything from Trent Falcon."

"What!" Hank snapped. "You mean that was the sister of the asshole who killed my father? God, I wish I had known that when she was standing in front of me. I would've given her a piece of my mind and then kicked her ass out of here."

Ridge's eyes shot back up to his cousin. "No, you wouldn't have. I gave up Jaleena because of your father. I was going to ask Jaleena to marry me, but I didn't because of Uncle Billy's views about interracial dating.

"He asked me to choose between him and Jaleena. I wasn't sure if he was going to make it back then, so I gave up the best thing in my life for him. He didn't think Jaleena was worthy of me. He told me that he wasn't sure someone like Jaleena should be my wife. I wanted to start a family with her and it never happened. Now, I'm alone and Uncle Billy is dead."

"Are you telling me Dad didn't think you could have the perfect family with Jaleena? What's wrong with you? I loved him, but I wouldn't have ever given up the woman I loved because of him. I've known for years how he felt about interracial dating, and that's why I never told him about some of my black girlfriends. I was an adult and he wasn't going to run my life. You shouldn't have allowed him to do that to you."

Sighing, Ridge ran his fingers through his hair as he thought about the mistake he had made with Jaleena. "I thought he loved me all these years, but I guess I was wrong. He only wanted to control me and when things weren't going his way he guilted me into doing something I shouldn't have. I'm ashamed for listening to him, but I'm even more ashamed of myself."

Ridge walked across the room and fell down into one of the chairs behind him and dropped his head into his hands.

"Ridge, I never…" Hank's voice trailed off as Ridge's held up his hand.

"Don't...I'm not in the mood for it. Just go. I need some peace and quiet for a few minutes."

He heard Hank open the door and go back into the office. He wasn't going to allow Hank to tell him anything about Jaleena. His father had taken her out of his life the first time, but it wasn't going to happen again. She came by to see him for a reason, and he was going to find out what.

He stretched his legs out in front of him. He turned over the envelope in his hands a few times before he opened it and pulled out the letter. Taking a deep breath, Ridge started reading what Trent had written to his sister. The more he read the words in front of him, the angrier he became until he balled up the paper and tossed it over towards the front desk.

"That son of a bitch!" Ridge snapped. "He targeted Uncle Billy on purpose and I lost Jaleena because of it. I swear if he wasn't already in jail I would make sure that his ass would have ended up there."

God, he had to go and see Jaleena. She had to know the reason why he had broken her heart. Maybe they could work through the past and get back together. He was willing to work past anything if she only gave him another chance to prove himself.

Getting up from the chair, Ridge made his way over Trent's letter but stopped when he spotted a white envelope lying on the floor in front of the desk. Why hadn't he noticed it when he was talking to Hank earlier? Bending down, he picked it up and turned it over in his hands a couple of times.

"Where did this come from?" He opened it up and several pictures dropped into his hands. He flipped through them and his heart caught at the sight of the beautiful baby boy.

Turning the first picture over, he saw the name *Aden Falcon* on the back and he knew the baby boy was his.

Why hadn't Jaleena told him she was pregnant? Did she come to tell him about his son today and got scared before she could get the words out? Well, he wasn't going to let the past rule his life anymore. He was going to be a part of his son's life, and if Hank or anyone else had a problem with it so be it.

"I'm going to do everything I can to win back Jaleena's love and be a part of Aden's life."

Chapter Twenty-Seven

The doorbell rang for a third time as Jaleena hurried to it before the person on the other side woke up Aden. It had taken her almost an hour to get him to sleep. Usually he was a pretty good baby and went to sleep as soon as she put him in his crib, but tonight for some reason he was a little fussier.

"Hold on, I'm coming," she said as she opened the door, stunned to find Ridge. "What are you doing here?"

She would never have guessed in a million years that he would be here, especially after he read Trent's letter. Maybe he came here to give her a piece of his mind, and she couldn't fault him at all. Her brother played a part in his uncle's death, so she would take anything he had to tell her.

"This is why I'm here," he answered.

Jaleena watched as Ridge pulled something from his back pocket and held it up in front of her. It was a picture of Aden.

How in the hell did he get that picture? They were in her purse the last time she looked at them, inside her car in front of his business. She was going to tell him about Aden, but he hadn't been there. Shit! They must have fallen out when she took out Trent's letter and gave it to his cousin.

"Ridge...I don't—"

"Jaleena, May I see him? Please... He's see my son... *please.*"

Stepping back, she waved Ridge inside the house and closed the door behind him. She wouldn't deny him the chance to see him son. Ridge coming here didn't mean anything was different between them. She couldn't let him know how excited she was to see him again after being apart for so long.

"I didn't realize I had lost those when I came to see you earlier," she admitted.

"You were there to see me. Why?" he asked, turning around to look at her.

"I had to apologize to you for what my brother did, and give you his letter. I couldn't keep that heaviness in my heart. What Trent did was wrong and I wanted to make things right," she said.

"I know getting shot is what played a part in your uncle dying. I was sorry to hear about that, I know how much you loved him. I had the pictures in my purse to show you. I guess they fell out when I pulled out the letter while I was talking to Hank."

"I'm glad they did or I wouldn't have ever known about Aden," Ridge said, shoving the picture back into his pocket. "Can I see him now?"

"Follow me." Jaleena turned in the direction of her bedroom with Ridge at her heels. She pushed opened the door and went over to the crib at the foot of her bed. "I'm redoing his nursery, so he's in here with me until I finish it."

"Ridge, this is your son, Aden Falcon," Jaleena told him then took a step back from the crib.

He looked down in the crib at his sleeping son. Tears filled his eyes as he ran an index finger down his son's baby smooth cheek. He had only known his little boy for a few seconds and he was already in love with him. No, he wasn't about to lose him or Jaleena again. The two of them were his family.

"You could have told me about him," he whispered softly so he wouldn't wake up Aden.

"I know, and I tried several times, but I would always get scared at the last minute. It was easy for you to reject me for your Uncle Billy, and I wasn't going to let you do that my son. I had to protect him and that is what I did, and I would do it again and again. He comes first in my life now."

"Our son," Ridge corrected, looking at her. "I love you and I would have been thrilled to find out you were carrying my child. I should have been there when he was born."

"You didn't have time to take care of a pregnant ex-girlfriend and Billy at the same time. You made your choice and I made mine. We both have to deal with it now. I'm doing well, so you don't have to worry about us."

"Baby, I know that I shouldn't have let my uncle pressure me like that. I'm so sorry. I have thought about you every day. You don't know how many times I drove past *Talk of the Town* and wanted to come in. I just couldn't work up the nerve because of what I had done to you. Please let me back into your life. I love you more than anything in this world. I want to watch our son grow up."

Jaleena wanted to toss Ridge out on his ass and tell

him never to come back, but she loved him too much. She hated being without him ever since Aden had been born. It would serve him right if she made him beg to be with her, yet she couldn't do it. She could hear the love that he had for her in his voice.

"Ridge, I love you, too," she confessed.

"God, Jaleena. I don't know what I'd have done if you pushed me out of your life and my son's life." Ridge wrapped her in his arms. "I know this may sound crazy to you since we just got back together, but I'm going to do it anyway.

"Jaleena Falcon, I love you and Aden with every fiber that I have in me. Will you end the misery I've been in for the past year and become my wife?"

"Yes, I'll marry you. Nothing will make me happier in the world than to bring in the New Year with you as my fiancée," she answered with a huge smile on her face.

Ridge lifted her up and planted a kiss on her mouth. "I think we should celebrate our upcoming wedding, don't you?"

He carried her over to her bed at the other side of the room. Ridge slowly slid her down his hard body until her feet touched the carpet. He pulled her tight against his body and slid his fingers through her hair, tilting her head back until she was staring up into his eyes.

"I really do love you, Jaleena," Ridge confessed. "You're beautiful, intelligent, and hot as hell. I've never thought about a woman as much as I did you when I lost you.

"I know we might have done things a little backwards by making love so soon when we first met, but we got a beautiful son from it that I already love. Please tell me that you are out on the ledge with me. I couldn't handle it if something tore us apart again before we got married. I spent last New Year's without you, but I can't spend another one. Are you really going to marry me?" he asked as a worried frown etched across his forehead.

※

Jaleena's heart jumped in her chest. She couldn't believe what she was hearing. This afternoon she was apprehensive about going to see Ridge. After she had read Trent's letter she wasn't sure how he might react. It was a huge step on her part to take it to his business and leave it there for him to read. Some people might not have been strong enough to handle the truth that her brother had written in that letter from prison.

Now, here Ridge was standing right in front of her telling her *again* how much he loved her. God, her life truly couldn't get any better right now. It felt amazing to know he felt the same way even after so much time had passed since they last saw each other.

Standing on her tiptoes, she brushed her lips across Ridge's firm, kissable mouth and moved back before he could deepen the kiss. She wanted to get everything out in the open before they made love. She didn't want any more secrets or lies between them. This was their second chance and she didn't want it ruined by anything.

"I don't think you've a thing to worry about, Mr. Taylor. I'm right out there on the ledge right next to you holding your hand. I won't let you be there without me. I love you way too much to ever allow that to happen."

Jaleena gasped as Ridge grabbed a fistful of her hair and turned her head, then worked his tongue down the side of her neck before nibbling at her skin. He ran his hand down her back and grabbed a handful of her ass, pressing her against his hard cock. His mouth slowly made its way down her body until it paused at her hard nipple poking through her thin t-shirt.

"Ridge," she moaned as he planted a kiss on her breasts.

"What, baby?" he whispered against the fabric as his other finger moved to play with her other nipple. "Is there something you want...?"

Her body jumped at the sound of her shirt being ripped and the touch of his rough fingers as they tugged as her nipples. She bit down on her bottom lip to keep from screaming as his thumb teased the nipple over and over—she didn't think she could take it anymore. She felt a tingling start in her stomach and work its way down to her pussy. He was almost like a drug to her and she couldn't make it without her fix.

"Tell me again that you love me," he demanded, lifting his mouth from her breasts.

Jaleena blinked a couple of times to clear her head, then looked at him in the eye. She knew he had asked her something again, but she wasn't quite sure what it was. "Huh?"

Smiling, Ridge made quick work of her shirt and shorts until she was standing completely naked in front of him. He ran his hands over her body, only pausing to brush his thumb over her pussy.

"I want to hear how much you love me," he whispered, staring into her eyes. "If there's something you want from me, tell me and I will give it to you."

"I love you, Ridge Taylor, more than anything in this world. You only have one house call tonight and it's me," Jaleena said, reaching for the hem of Ridge's shirt. She slowly tugged it over his head. She flung it behind them and it landed on top of a lampshade, but she didn't care. All she wanted to do was get him completely naked.

"I guess you answered my question," he chuckled as he picked her up and carried her over to the bed.

Ridge laid her down and took a step back. She watched as he quickly got rid of his clothes until he was standing naked in front of her. Jaleena didn't have time to admire his body again because he quickly closed the distance between them and lifted her up as he sat down on the mattress.

Spreading his thighs made his cock stand up proudly from his body before he lifted her to straddle him, then buried himself deep inside of her pussy. They both groaned at the same time as his thickness filled her tightness. Grasping her hips, he jerked and went even deeper, if that was possible.

"OhMyGod...yes," Jaleena moaned, rocking her hips against him. "You feel so good and thick."

"I think you're the one who feels amazing, sweetheart," he growled, holding her hips tighter as he continued thrusting inside of her pussy.

"I'm so glad you're here with me."

"Show me how glad you are," Ridge demanded.

Arching her back, she pressed her legs against the side of his hard thighs and began riding his cock hard and fast. She mewled as his hands reached up and touched her breasts, pulling at her nipples.

Jaleena hadn't been touched like this in such a long time, and the feel of Ridge's calloused hands on her body was doing things to her body that she had missed. She held her breath as his fingers continued to play with her nipples while his hard cock thrust in and out of her body. She moved her hips, trying to keep up with his hard, powerful movements, but it felt like he was so deeper inside of her—like the tip of his erection was brushing against her womb.

She sighed as his warm tongue licked at her swollen nipples before drawing one inside of his hot mouth and sucking hard. For a moment all words escaped her and Ridge concentrated on making love to her breasts while his dick reacquainted with her pussy.

One of his hands left her breasts and slid around her back, cupping her ass. He squeezed it before giving her a light slap, making her grip his cock tighter. The sensation shot even more pleasure through her body until she felt like she was about to explode.

"Your body is so fucking beautiful. I could touch it for the rest of my life and never get tired. God, I don't know how I made it think long without you, baby," he whispered against her breasts. "I promise you that we are going to make up for lost time."

Suddenly, Ridge flipped them over so her back was against the mattress. He spread her thighs in a wide V and pulled his cock all the way out until only the tip was left before shoving it back into her. She laid there trying to regain some sort of control, but what he did to her was just too much. He was controlling her body like no other man had done before, and she loved it. He was showing her who was the boss and she couldn't have told him to stop if her life depended on it. His fingers were holding onto her waist hard, but she didn't care because the pleasure was just too good…she wasn't about to tell him to stop!

Jaleena didn't have time to think before her back arched off the bed. Digging her nails into Ridge's back, her body clenched around his cock as her orgasm suddenly hit her and she screamed as it tore through her body.

"Oh, fuck," Ridge growled in a deep voice as sweat

poured from his body down onto his hers. "Baby, I need more...I'm almost there, but I need to be deeper inside of you. Taking her legs, he tossed them over his shoulders as he worked his cock in and out of her at a frenzied pace.

Seconds later, he screamed her name as his release tore through his hard, muscular body.

※

"I think we should take a quick twenty-minute nap, so I can make love to you again," Ridge whispered against the back of her neck as they snuggled up against each other in bed. One of his thick legs was tossed over hers as his hand cupped one of her breasts.

"I mean, it is New Year's Day and I can't think of a better way to start the morning, can you?"

He planted a kiss on the back of her neck when Aden decided to break the mood by crying his lungs out.

"I think your son doesn't care that it's three o'clock in the morning on New Year's Day. I think he has other plans. It's probably time for a diaper change. Would you like to do it?" Jaleena asked as she untangled her body from Ridge's and glanced at him over her shoulder. She got out of the bed and found Ridge's shirt on the floor. She slipped it over her head and walked towards the crib.

"If that means I get to spend time with my son, of course I want to do it. It's about time he gets used to seeing his daddy's face," Ridge said, getting out of the bed. He snatched his pants off the floor and slid them on as she made her way over to Aden. Just as she was about to reach from him, Ridge brushed her hands away and picked Aden up out of his crib.

Jaleena watched as her son stopped crying to study the

new person holding him. "I think he knows who you are."

"Do you really?" Ridge asked, looking from Aden to her.

"Of course, that's the reason he stopped crying. Now, let me get his stuff and I can teach you Diaper Changing 101."

Epilogue

Sitting in the rocking chair, Ridge glanced back over at the bed, smiling at his sleeping fiancée. Jaleena had been so worn out from their lovemaking that she hadn't even heard their son when had he woke up again, wanting some attention.

He looked down at his handsome son in his arms and couldn't keep his heart from swelling with even more love for the bundle of joy in his arms. For the past year, he had fallen into the dull routine of living without any passion or purpose because he had lost Jaleena. Now, he was blessed to have her back along with this beautiful baby. He never knew true love could feel like this at all.

Aden wrapped his tiny hands around his heart the second Ridge saw him sleeping inside of his crib, and he had to thank someone he hated for giving him a family. If Trent hadn't sent that letter from prison to his sister, he would have never known anything about Aden. Jaleena might have told him in time, but he couldn't have been sure and he wouldn't have blamed her if she hadn't.

Not after the way he had dumped her so coldly just to please his Uncle Billy.

He was getting a second chance and he wasn't about to mess it up for anything in the world. Few people got a do-over with the loves of their lives, and he would make damn sure nothing came between him and Jaleena again.

He loved her too much to ever spend another moment away from her and his son. As soon as she woke up he would suggest that they move in with him. His place had enough room for all three of them, and Aden's nursery would be something envied by all of the other babies in the neighborhood. He loved his son dearly and from this day on he only planned to give him and Jaleena the best out of life.

"Ridge, what are you doing? Is everything okay?"

Glancing over at the bed, he found Jaleena wide awake, sitting up in the bed looking at him. "Is there something wrong with Aden?"

He glanced down at his sleeping son and brushed a lock of hair off his forehead. "No, everything is absolutely perfect. I was just watching him sleep. It's the most beautiful sight in the world. I could do it every night for the rest of my life and never get tired of it."

"I know. Sometimes I just walk over there and stare at him inside of his crib wondering how I ever got so lucky to have him."

"I think meeting Aden tonight is the second best thing that ever happened to me," he said, staring at the woman he loved more than anything in this world.

Jaleena stared at him from across the room. "What's the best thing?" she asked.

"The day I walked into *Talk of the Town* and saw you,"

Ridge confessed. "I knew my life would forever be changed the moment our eyes connected and it was."

The End

About the Author

The Queen of Tease: If you want to read interracial romance stories that leaves you panting for more and turning the pages faster than you can read them. Marie is for you.

After reading her first "dirty" book as a teenager, Marie knew she had to become a writer. She started writing a few years ago because she wanted to reach for her dream. She writes her characters so her fans will believe in the Happily Ever After. She loves collecting bear figurines and reading a HOT book when she gets the chance.

Find out more about Marie here:
Official Site: http://marierochelle.weebly.com/
Official Blog: http://shopdiva28.blogspot.com/
Yahoo group: http://groups.yahoo.com/group/marie_rochelle/
Yahoo discussion group: http://groups.yahoo.com/group/MarieRochelle2/?yguid=289462859

CPSIA information can be obtained at www.ICGtesting.com
Printed in the USA
LVOW10s2121170914

404638LV00001B/17/P